She caught her breath as her heart lurched slightly. "You're very good at this, aren't you?"

"Sending flowers?" he teased.

"Seduction… I'm thinking you must have had lots of practice," she mused.

"Some, but there's no need to be jealous, sweetheart. You have my undivided attention now."

"You talk a good game. I hope you live up to expectations."

"I promise you won't be disappointed, princess," he vowed huskily.

D0834688

AMANDA BROWNING still lives in the house where she was born, in England. The third of four children—her sister being her twin—she enjoyed the rough-and-tumble of life with two brothers as much as she did reading books. Writing came naturally as an outlet for a fertile imagination. The love of books led her to a career in libraries, and being single allowed her to take the leap into writing for a living. Success is still something of a wonder, but allows her to indulge in hobbies as varied as embroidery and bird-watching.

The
SEDUCTION BID

AMANDA BROWNING

BACHELOR TYCOONS

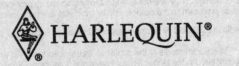

HARLEQUIN®

TORONTO • NEW YORK • LONDON
AMSTERDAM • PARIS • SYDNEY • HAMBURG
STOCKHOLM • ATHENS • TOKYO • MILAN • MADRID
PRAGUE • WARSAW • BUDAPEST • AUCKLAND

If you purchased this book without a cover you should be aware that this book is stolen property. It was reported as "unsold and destroyed" to the publisher, and neither the author nor the publisher has received any payment for this "stripped book."

ISBN 0-373-80593-4

THE SEDUCTION BID

First North American Publication 2000.

Copyright © 1999 by Amanda Browning.

All rights reserved. Except for use in any review, the reproduction or utilization of this work in whole or in part in any form by any electronic, mechanical or other means, now known or hereafter invented, including xerography, photocopying and recording, or in any information storage or retrieval system, is forbidden without the written permission of the publisher, Harlequin Enterprises Limited, 225 Duncan Mill Road, Don Mills, Ontario, Canada M3B 3K9.

All characters in this book have no existence outside the imagination of the author and have no relation whatsoever to anyone bearing the same name or names. They are not even distantly inspired by any individual known or unknown to the author, and all incidents are pure invention.

This edition published by arrangement with Harlequin Books S.A.

® and TM are trademarks of the publisher. Trademarks indicated with ® are registered in the United States Patent and Trademark Office, the Canadian Trade Marks Office and in other countries.

Visit us at www.eHarlequin.com

Printed in U.S.A.

CHAPTER ONE

KARI MAITLAND was so hopping mad, she was ready to spit nails. The cause of this fury was an article printed in the newspaper presently crumpled in the tense grip of her right hand. The selfsame newspaper whose offices she now strode through so purposefully. The angry rat-tat-tat of her stilettos on the linoleum floor was an audible measure of the tempest brewing inside her. Heads would roll, or she would want to know the reason why.

Oblivious to the sudden silence her entrance generated, along with the raised heads and frozen figures of the staff, she cut a swathe through to the office which was her goal. Nobody attempted to stop her, for to a man they held the conviction that, had they tried, she could have hurled them clear across the cluttered room. Dressed though she was in a fashionably styled sapphire-blue suit, she looked like nothing so much as an avenging angel.

Not in the least interested in the impression she was creating, Kari fixed her eye firmly on the male figure she could see through the window of the door. Lounging in the chair behind the desk, he had his feet propped comfortably on the window sill. The sight aggravated her to no end. She had found her friend Sarah in tears because of this man, and he couldn't care less about the mayhem he had caused!

Poor Sarah had worked so hard to put the scandal her father had created behind her. Now that she had made something of her life, and found a man she could love and trust, the editor of this…scandal-sheet had seen fit to resurrect it all again!

Anger tightened her face as she thought of her friend, but that couldn't hide the sheer stunning beauty of it. Today her blonde hair was caught back in an intricate plait which showed her swan neck to perfection. She had a fine English rose complexion which she had inherited from her mother. The translucent porcelain skin, tinged with just a hint of damask, was stretched over cheek-bones which were fine to the point of fragility. Her eyes, long-lashed and deeply blue, generally greeted the world with genuine warmth, and her mouth was a gentle curve which easily tilted into a smile.

Not today, however. The only emotion in her eyes was a fulminating anger. She thought of Sarah, and her lips tightened. Arriving at her friend's apartment for their weekly get-together over lunch, it hadn't taken Kari more than one glance to know her friend was upset, and scarcely more time to discover why. That damned article. Typically, Sarah hadn't wanted to make a fuss, but Kari couldn't let it go. Somebody had to be taken to task, and she was just the person to see that they were.

Having reached the office unopposed, she didn't bother to knock but sailed right in. From this vantage point she could see that the man at the desk had his eyes shut, and she spared a second to study him. He was an unedifying sight. His thick dark hair was an unruly mess, and he was wearing what appeared to be a dress suit. A slept-in dress suit, if she wasn't much mistaken. Her original anger was instantly bolstered by scorn, and without a qualm she slammed the door shut.

'What the hell?'

Lance Kersee came awake with a jerk that sent a jolt of pain shooting through the roof of his skull. His head shot round. Bloodshot grey eyes blinked open and locked blearily onto the face of a Botticelli angel. He frowned. Correction, a very angry Botticelli angel who looked as if there was a very nasty smell in the room, and it was emanating from him. Not exactly the sort of reaction he was used to getting from women—they generally wanted to get to know him better. Notwithstanding, he responded instinctively, giving her the once-over with a practised eye. She was taller than average, about five feet eight or nine barefoot, and curved in all the right places. There was a classy, refined look about her that hinted at old money. Without doubt she was the most stunning woman he had seen for a long while, and those legs... Hell, they just kept on going. His interest was instantly aroused, until he connected with her expression again, then he winced, closing his eyes. Great, just what he needed in his condition. A golden-haired virago breathing fire at him!

Damn, but he could do with some coffee! He'd been forced to take the red-eye because he had missed the flight he had intended to catch, and the result was every bit as bad as he had expected. Now this... Ordinarily, he would have done his best to soothe her anger and find out what was going on, but having had very little sleep in the last forty-eight hours he was in no mood to be charming.

'Have you ever heard of knocking and waiting to be invited in? Or is that only for the *hoi polloi*?' he growled, rubbing a hand over his eyes and wishing they didn't feel as if they had a ton of grit in each of them.

Kari observed these signs of frailty unmoved, and tossed the mangled newspaper down onto the desk with all the force of her anger. 'I presume you're the editor of this rag,' she said in a voice cold enough to freeze water from twenty paces.

Lance frowned at her, and instantly regretted even that small movement. Damn it, there had to be some aspirin around here somewhere—if he dared move to search for it. With more care he looked from her to the door with its declaration that the occupant of this room was the editor. Which it would have been had his cousin been present. Lance was only making use of it in his absence.

He was actually a financial expert, a troubleshooter who was called in to save businesses both small and large. Sometimes by ruthless measures, and sometimes by a little judicial tweaking. He had developed quite a reputation over the years for his high success rate. He was in Maine to have dinner with an old friend, and had taken the opportunity to drop in to see Nick on his way north. Unfortunately Nick had had to attend a meeting, so while Lance waited for him to return he had taken the opportunity to sleep off some of his jet lag.

None of which this angry beauty was aware of. She had made a reasonable assumption, but a wrong one. He knew he ought to put her straight before she went any further, but a spark of devilment kept him from correcting her. He justified this lack of courtesy easily. She'd burst in without a by-your-leave, so she could just stew for a while longer. He'd tell her in his own good time.

'You can presume what you damned well please, so long as you do it quietly,' he told her shortly, and watched her cross her arms. He'd just bet she was tapping an elegantly shod foot, too. She certainly was a passionate creature. It was a shame she didn't channel it into something infinitely more pleasurable—something the two of them could enjoy.

The thought surprised him. He wasn't generally given to fantasising about women in the middle of a working day, but he wasn't working right now. He had a startlingly erotic vision of her wrapping those long legs around him in the heat of passion. He couldn't recall ever being so swiftly aroused by a woman, and he had known his fair share. Angry or not, she packed one hell of a sensual punch.

Unaware of his train of thought, Kari was indeed tapping her foot. It was either that or throw something at him. Of all the nerve! He expected consideration whilst giving none. How utterly typical! 'By that I can take it you *are* responsible for this,' she went on scathingly, pointing to the offending paper.

Lance carefully uncurled his long-legged, leanly muscular frame from its comfortable position, placing his elbows on the desk and resting his chin on his hands. It was the only way of making sure his head stayed on his shoulders. He shouldn't have drunk so much yesterday, but it wasn't every day that a man's best friend got married. Rubbing a hand wearily over his face, he tested the degree of stubble on his chin. He badly needed a shave, but suspected the noise would half kill him. His eyes hurt when he tried to read the article, and he abandoned the attempt. It wasn't his business anyway.

'I take it there's something on your mind, princess?' he challenged dryly, and could tell his tone rankled by the way she bristled. He was fascinated by the colour her eyes took on when they flashed angrily. They almost became violet. He was tempted to goad her just to watch it happen again.

Kari looked him over with mounting scorn. What a sorry excuse for a man! He was nothing but a hack, with bleary eyes, unshaven chin and rumpled clothes. She could think of only one reason for such a state of dilapidation. 'You're drunk!' she charged distastefully, not doubting it for a second.

Now that was taking the war to the enemy. The instant she got personal, every instinct Lance possessed demanded he fight back. A glint of angry amusement lighting up his eyes, he sat back with the exaggerated care of someone who had travelled this road before. Which was far from true. He had overindulged on a half-dozen memorable occasions during his thirty-four years on this earth. It did not make him a dipsomaniac.

'Correction. I was drunk, angel. Now, I am merely

hung over. I was sleeping it off when you made your…grand entrance,' he replied sardonically.

If he was trying to tweak her conscience, he was doomed to disappointment. 'My heart bleeds for you,' she scorned.

He smiled grimly. OK, if she wanted to play hardball, he was her man. He had cut his teeth in boardrooms which were no place for the squeamish. She was doing her best to annoy him, so he would see how she liked receiving some of her own medicine.

'You know, for a beautiful woman, you've got a damned sour tongue, princess,' he countered, and was amused to see the colour ebb from her face. Just as he thought, the lady did not like that.

Indeed she didn't, but not for any reason he would ever be able to imagine. Kari had been caught on the raw. The comment snagged a wound which would never completely heal. In a kind of time warp, she heard again the harsh voice of another stranger registering his dislike of her sharp tongue. His method of dealing with it had been as swift as it had been painful. Hastily she closed the door on the memory. She wasn't going to think about that time.

'I speak as I find. If you sow the wind, you must reap the whirlwind. The behaviour of the press means it doesn't deserve any special consideration,' she returned icily.

'That's a rather sweeping statement, wouldn't you say?' Lance challenged shortly, and wasn't surprised when she tilted her head and sniffed eloquently. Her cool smile had a superior quirk which made him itch to remove it. He couldn't recall any woman annoying him this much, and that included his sister.

'Have you ever heard of moral responsibility? I don't think so. I seriously doubt you even know what decency is.'

The little madam! A nerve ticked in his jaw, a sure sign, had she known it, that he was beginning to lose his cool, something he never normally did with a woman. This was turning out to be a day of firsts. First he had had to take a flight any intelligent person would avoid, and now she was this close to making him lose his temper.

'Oh, I know what decency is, princess. It's making me give you a warning, even though I know it won't be appreciated. Be advised, my temper is on a very short fuse right now. It won't take much to set it off,' he gritted out warningly, fixing her with a gimlet eye. In the boardroom, it would have made strong men blanch, but this woman apparently had nerves of steel. Despite his annoyance, he found himself being impressed.

Kari ignored the warning just as he'd assumed she would, and instead regarded him down her delightfully proportioned nose, taking in all the evidence of the morning after. Lord, how she hated people who abused power, and this man was one of the worst.

'You know, I always thought the phrase ''gutter press'' referred to a level of journalism. I had no idea a prerequisite for the job was to actually look as if you'd been crawling in the gutter too!'

Lance raised a pair of straight black eyebrows at that little gem. The woman was either very brave, or too dense to be afraid. Either way, she was proving herself a right royal pain, and his lips pursed in a sardonic wince. 'Have you noticed how good advice is so very rarely taken? You must like living dangerously. Do you eat glass for breakfast, you sharp-tongued little shrew?'

She couldn't help catching her breath because she was so very rarely on the receiving end of such comments. But there again, she wasn't in the habit of lambasting strangers either. This man simply rubbed her up the wrong way, and, as Russ had been fond of saying, she charged in like a terrier. With more spirit than good sense.

'At least I don't take my breakfast from a bottle! But then, in order to write the sleaze you do, you'd have to view the world through the bottom of a glass!'

The slur brought Lance to his feet, a rash move which drew a groan from him and he glared at her balefully until his head stopped thudding. The damn woman didn't know where to stop! 'Princess, were you born reckless, or is it something you've perfected over the years? Right now I'm just moderately annoyed. Don't get me mad.'

Kari never had responded well to threats, and she placed her hands on the cluttered desktop and thrust a belligerent chin his way. 'Oh, dear, have I hurt your feelings? Now you know how it feels to be on the receiving end of the sort of trash you and your sort dish out!'

Lance's teeth snapped together audibly. He had

had it. There were limits to what he would take from anyone, woman or man. 'Have you finished?'

Her blue gaze glittered with dislike. A log-jam of anger finally broke free, and there was no way she could stop it gushing forth. 'I've only just begun, you third-rate hack. You muckraking—' Her words were brought to an abrupt halt, for with an agile movement which more than hinted at latent power, and despite his condition, her protagonist rounded the desk to tower over her threateningly.

'All right! No more Mr Nice Guy!' Lance snarled, aware in the recesses of his mind that he was over-reacting and then some, but there was something about her that pushed him to the edge.

Kari held her ground, even if his sudden move had surprised her. His size gave her a jolt. Lord, he was big! Well over six foot. Now he was standing, she had a totally different view of him and all of a sudden it made her mouth go dry. For a man the worse for drink, he was nerve-tinglingly impressive. His shoulders were broad, filling the coat to perfection. Even in the state he was in, he literally oozed male-ness. She felt its potency like a blow, and her stom-ach flip-flopped. He had the most piercing grey eyes, despite their redness. Deep inside her something stirred in response, and her heart lurched in shock as she recognised the signs of sexual awareness.

She hadn't found herself responding to a man this swiftly in all her twenty-eight years. Oh, she had been attracted to a few, for she was only human, but never as strongly as this. The man obviously had something the others hadn't. The discovery did not thrill her. He was the last man she wanted to be attracted to!

Deploring her senses' lack of discrimination, she lifted her chin another notch and ignored everything except her anger.

'You call this Nice Guy? Where did you learn it? At the Thugs School of Charm?' she sneered disdainfully, hoping she hadn't given herself away. The last thing she needed was for this oaf to know how he affected her.

She would have been disappointed. Lance had seen the flare of awareness in her eyes before she had muffled it with her anger, and it had sent a shock wave through him. So, she felt it too, this powerful attraction. However, before he could decide what he was going to do about it, she let rip with her next verbal salvo, distracting him. He had to give it to her, she had spirit. He almost laughed. He probably would have done if he hadn't got the mother of all headaches, and she hadn't irritated the hell out of him.

'I got it the same place you did, sweet lips,' he drawled mockingly. 'You didn't learn such charming turns of phrase from any fancy finishing school,' he continued, hell-bent on scoring a point or two of his own. 'Sounds like you've been spending too much time in the wrong company. Where did you broaden your education? In the garage and stables of the fancy home you live in?'

His words knocked the air clean out of her, and it seemed to Kari that he had an uncommon knack of reminding her of things which she was doing her best to forget. For one agonising instant she was spirited back to that other time and place where the air was hot and filled with the sound of whickering horses, and all was terror and pain. She shuddered and dragged herself back to the present.

'That's just the sort of reasoned argument I'd expect from you. You're just another cheap hack who takes potshots at those better off than yourself out of pure sour grapes. If you can't join them, beat them!' she exclaimed, but her voice carried the merest tremor.

Hearing it, Lance narrowed his fine grey eyes thoughtfully. The expressions flitting over her face had been very revealing, and he wondered if she was aware of it. Probably not. Whatever he had said to send her thoughts to where they had been, it was obviously not a nice place to be. When she came back, there were shadows in her eyes he honestly didn't enjoy seeing. Especially as he had been responsible for putting them there. The lady had demons, and much to his surprise he had a quixotic impulse to slay them for her. Another first, and one he could do nothing about. Though it felt wrong to ignore it, he had no choice.

'I am neither a hack, nor do I come cheap.' He wasn't any sort of hack, and he knew he ought to tell her so, but, as much as he was attracted to her, the woman had ticked him off too much. If she were to stop insulting him, or the person she thought he was, for five minutes, he might consider changing his mind. Unfortunately neither event seemed likely. A fact she confirmed in the next few seconds.

'They pay you well to write lies that destroy people's lives, do they? Blood money, no doubt!' she exclaimed and held his gaze accusingly.

Lance bared his teeth in a grin. She was something else. There was nothing of her. She was so slight a puff of wind would blow her away, but she was full of grit. Five-feet eight-inches of feisty womanhood. Annoyance aside, he could admit her fervour was impressive. Nevertheless, it would give him the greatest pleasure to pick her up and toss her out on her precious little behind!

'Princess, you're getting awful close to losing one of your nine lives. Why don't you back off whilst you still have the chance?' he advised softly, and anyone who knew him would have wisely taken the advice rather than risk the consequences. He was not known for giving quarter. A fact of which she was blissfully ignorant. Nor would it have made any difference if she weren't. Kari was a fighter, and would prefer to retreat from any fight bloody, but unbowed.

'I'm not leaving here until I get your promise to print an apology. That story is a scandal and you know it,' she refused doggedly.

'Do I?' he challenged pigheadedly, not in the least surprised. He knew very well the tone of the newspaper his cousin worked for. They argued about it constantly. He simply wasn't about to admit it to this little termagant.

Kari had expected no less a response, and looked him up and down witheringly. 'Well, naturally *you* wouldn't think so. You would have to have some moral principles. The person who would allow that article to be printed has no morals at all!'

In one of those strange quirks of fate, Lance found himself defending his cousin, when in actual fact he had thought the same thing more than once. However, he had started this and had to see it through.

'If you think being a woman allows you to insult me with impunity, you're on the wrong track, princess. I wouldn't take it from a man, and I certainly won't take it from you!'

Predictably, Kari refused to back down. 'What are you going to do, hit me?' she goaded. She wouldn't put anything past him.

Tempting as the thought was to dust her behind, Lance had been raised to treat women with respect. In his book, a man who struck a woman was a cowardly bully, taking unfair advantage of his superior strength. There were other, better ways to deal with an angry woman. Had they been anywhere else he would have hauled her into his arms and kissed her until her anger turned to something much more rewarding. Automatically his eyes dropped to her mouth. He wondered if her lips would soften beneath his the way he thought they might.

Not that he was about to find out. That was not the way to go in this situation. He would probably find himself in the emergency room needing stitches. Besides, there was more than one way to skin a cat.

'You're forgetting, I have other means at my disposal,' he informed her, inclining his head in the direction of the newspaper she had thrown down, the threat inherent in the gesture.

She didn't miss it, and it showed just how low he was! 'Print anything defamatory about me, and I'll sue!' she warned.

Lance shook his head, which proved to be a mistake for it protested violently. He closed his eyes, waiting for the world to settle down before responding. 'It wouldn't be defamatory. I pride myself on telling the truth.'

'Truth, as you see it, obviously means trampling over people's feelings in hobnailed boots.'

Damn it, didn't she ever wind down? Lance was heartily beginning to wish he hadn't allowed this situation to get so out of hand. But he wouldn't tell her the truth now if she paid him. 'Well, you see, people's feelings are awkward things. I dare say a thief wouldn't want his feelings hurt by having the truth told either.'

Kari forgot a lifetime's teaching and stamped her foot. 'It's not the same thing and you know it! That article was supposed to be about Sarah's engagement. There were only a couple of paragraphs about it, the rest you hijacked and used to dredge up the scandal about her father. He paid for what he did. You had no right bringing it all up again. It has no bearing on her. I want an apology. No, I demand one!'

'You demand one?' he repeated in a dangerously soft tone. Had she not chosen to use those words, he might well have reacted differently, but she did, and it pushed buttons he had almost forgotten existed.

His father's second wife had been a demanding woman, and it was Lance's belief that this had led to his father's early death. It was no wonder he did not respond well to demands.

'Honey, you may live in a world where your every demand is met, but that doesn't wash with me. I'll let you into another truth you won't like. The world doesn't revolve around you and your wants, and it would do you a great deal of good to come down off your high horse, stop demanding this or that, and start saying please like the rest of us peasants!'

'How dare you?' Tiny flags of colour tinted her cheeks, all the more painful because she knew he was right. It was the wrong tack to take.

'Quite easily. Your kind give me a pain,' he observed with patent dislike and returned to his chair. 'OK, princess, you've had your say, now it's my turn. You came in here uninvited, which means you know where the door is. Close it on your way out.' He underlined the dismissal by lifting his feet to the desk and closing his eyes.

Kari fumed impotently, knowing she had made a tactical error. 'You're despicable. You haven't heard the last of this. Our family stands for something around here.'

He uttered a short bark of laughter. 'I wondered when we'd get around to that. My family stands for something too,' he retorted.

'No doubt as a byword for everything cheap, tacky, sordid and underhand. A real name to be proud of!'

That was one jibe too many. 'Now you are finished. You can have the choice of leaving under your own steam or being thrown out, but out you most definitely are going.'

Kari glared at him futilely. She felt like screaming in frustration, but knew that nothing was going to get through to this man. 'I'm going. I should have known it was a waste of time to come. It's impossible to appeal to the finer feelings of someone who doesn't possess any!'

With that she turned to the door, jerking it open and nearly bowling over the man who had been poised to enter. Brushing past him without a glance, she strode through the office as angrily as she had when she'd arrived. The loathsome man. She hoped he tripped on that gutter of his and broke his neck.

Reaching the bank of elevators, she jabbed at the button, willing it to arrive quickly. All she wanted to do now was get out of there as quickly as possible. The elevator arrived and she stepped into it, allowing it to whisk her away from the man who had thwarted her at every turn. She never wanted to see him again as long as she lived!

CHAPTER TWO

HAVING stepped neatly out of harm's way, Nick Fraser did a double take on the departing woman, then strolled into his office. 'What did *she* want?' he asked his cousin curiously.

Lance swung his legs off the desk in a jerky movement, rose to his feet and began pacing backwards and forwards in the small space, swearing long and hard under his breath. He shot his cousin a narrow-eyed look as he passed him.

'She had a complaint and thought I was you,' he said darkly. 'If your ears weren't burning, they should have been. That was a lady with very definite feelings about you, and none of them good. You owe me one for running interference, Nick.'

'Why didn't you tell her who you were?' Nick asked, and to his amazement a faint wash of colour stole up Lance's neck.

'Because she never gave me the chance,' he exploded wrathfully, and not exactly truthfully. He could have told her, but had chosen not to. 'Later I would have been damned if I told her!'

Nick bit back a grin. 'Got you mad, did she?' he asked in amusement, and his cousin glared at him.

'That woman...' Lance began hotly, then, seeing the laughter on Nick's face, he stopped and took a steadying breath. Hands on hips, he stared at the empty doorway, beyond which the offices were once more a hive of industry. His anger faded like mist on a sunny day to be replaced by a strange, warm glow inside him. He shook his head and grinned suddenly. 'She was kind of magnificent, wasn't she?' he said with a wry laugh. Now that she was gone, the tilt of her chin and the angry glitter in her eyes became intriguing. He had never encountered anyone like her. What would it take, he wondered, to turn her growls into purrs?

'I only caught the tail-end of it, remember?' Nick remarked, grinning back.

'I've met company presidents with less guts. Believe me, Nick, she stood toe-to-toe with me and wouldn't give an inch. It gives me gooseflesh just to think about it,' Lance said in some awe. He felt, well, proud of her, even though he had been on the receiving end of her verbal punches.

'OK, *you* were impressed, but what about her? It seemed to me she wasn't too taken with you, buddy. What happened to the famous Kersee charm?'

'At the time, I didn't want to charm the little hellcat. I wanted to murder her,' he admitted ruefully. Half the time he had wanted to strangle her, and the other half he had spent wondering what it would be like to make love to her.

'And now? I take it you've changed your mind?' Nick enquired curiously, thinking he had never seen his cousin in this kind of mood before.

Lance thought of the way she had stood up to him, and knew it was that which impressed him most. She had been proud, fearless and loyal, giving as good as she got. Just as he had told Nick, she was magnificent. She had made him feel so many things in the space of no time at all, he knew she was something special. So special, he would be a fool if he let her get away. He had discovered over the years that there were times when you had to go with your instincts. This was one of those times.

He turned and looked at his cousin steadily. 'She's the one, Nick. She's the woman I'm going to marry,' he said with the utmost conviction.

Nick was absolutely poleaxed. 'What?' he croaked in disbelief.

Lance appreciated his shock. He must sound as if he'd lost his mind, but he knew he hadn't. As long as he could remember, he had lived with the conviction that he would know the woman he was going to marry the instant he met her. That was why none of his relationships had been serious. Though he hadn't realised it until this moment, suddenly he knew he was going to marry the woman who had just walked out of the office. She was the one. The woman he had been looking for all his life. He'd never been more certain of anything in his whole life.

'I'm going to marry her,' he repeated confidently.

'You're crazy!' Nick pronounced with a shake of his head, and Lance pulled a wry face.

'I've never felt saner in my life,' he disagreed, thinking of a pair of large blue eyes which had shot daggers at him. She would give him hell, but the other promise in her eyes would make it worth it.

Nick propped himself on the edge of his desk. 'I

can't believe I'm hearing this,' he said dazedly. 'Are you seriously telling me you've fallen for her?'

Lance hadn't actually thought of it in those terms, he only knew that she was different and he would be a fool if he let her get away. Now Nick mentioned it, though, he realised it was true. He was, to use his sister's term, smitten. She had exploded into his heart as she had exploded into the office. One instant he hadn't been aware of her existence, and the next... He couldn't imagine a life without her in it.

Sitting back down, he rubbed a hand around his neck as he absorbed the truth of it. She had ranted and raged at him, called him all the names under the sun, but all he had really wanted to do was take her in his arms and kiss her. If that wasn't love, he didn't know what was.

'Hook, line and sinker,' he conceded, without a single feeling of regret.

'But you've only known her, what...half an hour?' Nick spluttered.

Lance smiled. There was only one person he knew who would not be surprised, and that was his sister Rachel. He had told her about his conviction years ago, when she had teased him about all the women he dated. She hadn't teased him since. 'It only takes a minute when it's the right one,' he responded.

'Aren't you forgetting something? The lady wasn't interested in you,' Nick reminded him direly.

Lance rubbed a hand over his whiskery jaw. 'That does kind of put a spoke in it,' he agreed, though his eyes gleamed with anticipation. He thought about the glacial look in her eye, and knew he could melt it,

for she had given herself away. She was far from
being cold. The next time he saw her... 'Hell!' He
sat up with a jerk.

'What is it?' his cousin asked, frowning.

'I have no idea who she is,' Lance confessed, feeling his heart slam in his chest in sudden anxiety.
God, he didn't know anything about her, he realised,
and even through his alarm he heard Nick laughing.
He turned on him incredulously.

'That's priceless! You intend to marry her, but you
don't know who she is. What a hoot!'

Lance wasn't amused. 'You're asking for a black
eye,' he threatened.

'Lay a finger on me, and I won't tell you her
name,' Nick warned, and Lance's anger disappeared
as quickly as it had come.

'You know her?'

'I know of her. She was married to the son of a
former ambassador,' Nick explained.

Lance's brows rose questioningly. 'Was married?'

'Beautiful Kari is a widow. Her husband was
killed some years ago now.'

It surprised Lance to hear that she was a widow.
She looked too young to have been married and wid-
owed. 'Kari who?'

'Maitland. Kari Maitland.'

Lance was startled and his head shot round. 'Did
you say Maitland? The former ambassador's name
wouldn't be Robert Maitland, would it?' Surely he
couldn't be that lucky?

'It would indeed.'

Lance sat up straighter. 'Well, I'll be damned.'

'I wouldn't be at all surprised,' Nick rejoined smartly.

'It so happens I'm dining with Robert and his wife on Thursday night,' Lance revealed, stunned by the coincidence. He had met Robert and Georgia Maitland in Australia some years ago and had struck up a friendship with them. This was his first opportunity to meet up with them since Robert had retired from diplomatic service last year.

'You have the luck of the devil. Will she be there?'

'I have no idea,' Lance answered distractedly. His mind was absorbing the possibility. He experienced a rush of anticipation at the thought of seeing her again. This time the outcome was going to be different. When he saw something he wanted, he went after it, and he wanted Kari Maitland.

'She isn't going to be amused when she finds out you've made a fool of her,' Nick observed.

Lance knew it, but he refused to be negative. He wanted Kari Maitland for his wife, and he was used to getting what he wanted. 'She won't stay mad for long. We'll be married by Labour Day,' he returned confidently.

Nick groaned. 'You don't think you're being over-confident? She didn't look like a woman who was ready to fall into your arms.'

'I wasn't trying.' True, he didn't usually have to try much at all, but that was the challenge.

'We-ll, if anyone can do it, you can,' Nick agreed, warming to the idea. 'It won't be easy.'

Lance laughed. 'Good, I enjoy a challenge.'

'She has my sympathy,' Nick came back dryly. 'All the same, I'd keep her away from sharp knives and blunt instruments,' he added facetiously. 'That was a hell of a temper tantrum I caught the end of.'

Lance's smile was determined. 'Don't worry. I'm quite capable of taking care of myself and Kari Maitland.'

Catching sight of the newspaper which still lay accusingly on the desk, he smoothed it out and quickly read the offending article. His jaw tightened as he reached the end of it, and there was a nasty taste in his mouth. It was, without doubt, the worst piece of garbage he'd read in a long time, and then some. He felt a twinge of sympathy for the little fire-brand's friend.

Tossing the paper towards his cousin, Lance shot him a hard look. 'She was right about this, though, Nick. That article stinks,' he declared, reaching behind the chair for the flight bag he had brought with him.

Nick glanced at it. 'What do you want me to do? The owner chose the angle he wants the paper to take,' he returned as Lance stood up.

'You could try looking for another job, one more worthy of your talents. Failing that, you might care to print an apology.'

'That's never been done before.'

'Create a precedent. You'd win more friends than you lose,' Lance suggested as he shook the other man's hand. 'Thanks for the loan of the office, Nick. I needed the rest. The red-eye really knocked me out.'

'You're welcome,' Nick said, following him out. 'And I'll see what I can do about the article,' he added grudgingly.

Lance slapped him on the shoulder, then ambled over to the bank of elevators. Sighing, he pressed the button. The sooner he got to the hotel the better. He planned on having a long hot bath followed by an even longer sleep. The elevator arrived and he stepped inside, leaning back against the wall as it made its interrupted descent to the car park. His thoughts automatically drifted back to Kari Maitland. She was amazing. He admired her spirited defence of her friend, and, remembering it, he found himself grinning and shaking his head. Boy, did she know how to fight dirty! She had been a worthy opponent. She certainly hadn't been afraid of him.

A husky laugh escaped him. It wasn't going to be easy winning her round, but he knew he could do it. Though she didn't know it, Kari Maitland's days as a single woman were numbered.

Unaware of what was transpiring in her absence, Kari left the newspaper offices in a rage of disappointment. She had failed, and she hated failing. It wasn't any good telling herself she hadn't had a hope of winning. The truth was she had done everything wrong right from the very beginning. She stood by everything she had said, but she was intelligent enough to know she had wrecked her cause from the word go. She shouldn't have lost her temper. She had had every intention of playing it cool, but... God, he had just made her so angry!

Damn him, anyway. She hoped he had a hangover to end all hangovers!

Glancing at her watch showed her that she was way overdue back at the shop. She owned and ran an antiquarian book shop, and she had promised faithfully that she would not be late. Of course, that had been before she had found Sarah in tears. Nothing had gone right after that. She hurried to where she had parked the car, knowing the long trip home would make her later than ever, promising to make it up to Jenny somehow.

She had moved back to Brunswick almost five years ago because she hadn't been able to stay in the house she had shared with Russ after he had died. It had had too many memories—bad ones at the end. Luck had been on her side when the previous owner of the shop had decided to retire. She had used some of the money from the sale of their property to buy it, and a small house on the edge of town.

Buying the shop had given her life a purpose it had lost with Russ. She had qualified as a librarian and archivist at college, and it was a pleasure to actually use those skills in her work. She had one full-time assistant, Jenny, and two students, who came in a couple of days a week to help out.

Jenny was busy seeing to a customer when Kari entered the shop over half an hour later, and she waved to her as she went through to her office. She called Sarah the instant she sat down at her desk. As she waited for her friend to pick up the phone, she reran the encounter in her mind. Now that her temper had cooled, she looked at it more objectively. Doing so brought colour to her cheeks, and she closed her eyes, pressing a hand over them. Good Lord, she had said things which made her cringe, now that she was calm enough to remember them. The next instant she told herself not to be so silly. He had deserved every scornful remark she had made!

Inevitably, thinking of him brought other memories to mind, and she found it impossible not to recall how aware she had been of him. Her senses had come alive in a way that had been totally unexpected. For over four years no man had raised more than a passing interest in her, which had faded after a few dates. Today she had looked into a pair of fathomless grey eyes and all that had changed. Whatever power the man possessed, it had produced an intensity of physical awareness of him which had been stunning.

Not to mention immensely irritating. Why had it had to be him, of all people, who appealed to her senses so strongly? He was a man she had no respect for. How could she be drawn to him, when there were so many better men around? She had to have taken leave of her senses! She was mightily relieved there was little chance of her seeing him again.

The cessation of ringing at the other end of the line brought her back to the present.

'Sorry, Sarah, I blew it,' Kari puffed out frustratedly the minute she heard her friend's voice, sitting back in her chair and kicking off her shoes.

'Never mind. At least you tried,' Sarah Benton soothed down the line. Not many people had friends willing to put themselves out as Kari had.

'But it was so unfair!' Kari squawked, even

though she knew better than anyone how unfair life could be. She and Russ should have had years together, but instead he was dead and she was alone.

'I agree, and so does Mark. He rang just after you left.'

Hearing that, Kari perked up at once. 'And?' she urged, needing to know if Mark Taylor was as nice a man as she had always believed him to be. If he let Sarah down now...

Sarah laughed happily. 'He said he already knew all about my father. That if he was the sort of man to allow ancient history to bother him, he didn't deserve me. He said he loves me, and if I wanted to hear some real horror stories we could sit down some night and dig up his family skeletons!'

That brought a gurgle of delighted laughter from Kari. 'Good for him!'

'I'm so happy!' Sarah exclaimed, sounding joyful and tearful at the same time.

'You have every right to be,' Kari insisted, smiling broadly. Everything was going to be all right.

'I was an idiot to get so worked up,' Sarah confessed ruefully a moment later. 'It's just that my father...'

Kari grimaced feelingly. 'I know.' The past had a habit of returning to haunt her, too. Some things never went away.

'I'm not going to think about the past any more. I'm going to look forward, not back,' Sarah decided happily, and Kari smiled again.

'That's the spirit. You have everything to look forward to now.'

'I do, don't I?' Sarah agreed with a satisfied sigh.

'No thanks to me,' Kari muttered wryly, thinking of her abortive attempt. 'Talk about disaster!'

'Well, come on. Don't keep it to yourself. Tell me what happened,' her friend urged with lively curiosity.

Kari shifted uncomfortably in her seat. 'I did it all wrong,' she admitted dolefully, not wanting to go into the details.

Unfortunately, that was not enough for Sarah, who wanted the t's crossed and the i's dotted. 'In what way wrong?'

Knowing she was not about to get away with revealing less than the truth, Kari groaned and confessed. 'OK, if you must know, I got mad.' There, she had said it.

'Kari Maitland, are you telling me you blew your top?' Sarah charged in a tone of shock so obviously false, her friend sighed helplessly.

'Need you ask? It virtually ended up as a slanging match!' She could still scarcely credit it herself. She had gone way over the top, and that was so unlike her, despite her reputation for wading in where angels feared to tread. There was something about him which had rubbed her up the wrong way, leaving her spitting like a cat.

'Oh, dear!' Sarah responded faintly, patently holding back laughter.

'Don't you dare laugh! The man was impossible! A monster! You have no idea what he was like!' Kari exclaimed in self defence. 'It wasn't my fault!' The cry was a time-honoured one and got the expected reaction.

'Oh, Kari!' Sarah declared, bursting into irrepressible giggles.

'I know. I know.' Her temper had been a constant source of merriment for her friend. It wasn't that she lost it often, but simply that when she did the result was usually spectacular in its effect. Kari waited patiently for the laughter coming down the line to end before continuing. 'Can I take it the wedding goes ahead as planned?' she asked dryly.

'Absolutely. It's going to be perfect. I only intend to get married once, so I'm insisting on the works. Are you sure you won't be a bridesmaid?' she wheedled for the nth time, but Kari was adamant.

'I'm sorry, Sarah, but I can't.'

Her friend sighed, though she had known it was a vain effort. 'OK. Just you make sure you catch the bouquet, though. I'll be aiming it right at you.'

Kari felt her smile fade. She sat forward, fingers twisting the phone's cord into knots. 'You'll be wasting all that good luck. You know I'm never going to get married again.'

Marriage meant loving, and loving meant giving her heart. But her heart had been broken so badly, she hadn't been able to bear it, and she had locked it away where nothing could reach it. It had hurt too much to love and lose Russ. She was never going to lay herself open to that kind of pain again. She was never going to allow herself to love anyone. It was a risk she simply wasn't prepared to take.

At the other end of the line, Sarah had sobered

too. 'Oh, Kari, don't say that. You can't possibly be so certain. Why, a year from now, you could feel differently,' she insisted gruffly.

Kari stared at an exotic print hanging on the wall opposite her, but for once its beauty escaped her. A heavy weight seemed to have settled over her heart as she remembered how her dreams had all come crashing down. 'And a year after that I could lose everything. I can't put myself through that again, Sarah. I won't. It would kill me for certain,' she returned achingly, her throat so tight it hurt.

'It won't happen again, Kari. What happened was…a freak incident. You can't deny yourself another chance of happiness because of it,' Sarah returned swiftly, her own throat closing over with emotion.

Kari's expression was uncompromising. 'I'm happy with my life just the way it is,' she insisted firmly, and her friend sighed.

'Kari, have you ever asked yourself if Russ would approve of what you're doing?' Sarah asked gently, and Kari gasped in shocked surprise.

'What?' she demanded faintly, and at the other end of the line Sarah bit her lip but went on undaunted.

'I knew Russ, remember? He loved life. Wouldn't he have wanted you to find someone else, Kari?'

It was a second or two before Kari could find her voice, because she knew Sarah was right. Russ would have urged her to find someone else to love. But he wasn't the one who had been left alone and in pain. 'It's asking too much of me. Call it cowardice. Call it what you like, I just can't take that risk, Sarah.'

'But... Oh, Lord, I wish I knew what to say to persuade you,' Sarah protested despairingly.

Eyes closed, Kari ran her finger over the diamond-studded wedding band she still wore. 'There's nothing you can say. You know what it's like to love someone with all your heart, Sarah. I pray to God you never know what it's like to lose him,' she went on, barely audible, yet her friend heard and it brought tears to her eyes.

'I can only imagine what it must have been like,' she choked out.

'If you can, then you'll know why I can never, ever, risk going through anything like that again. It hurt too much, Sarah. It just...hurt too much.' The only way she could be sure of not being hurt was to keep her heart locked safely away.

It took a while for Sarah to answer, and she had to clear her throat first. 'I'm sorry. I promise I won't press you any more. Just tell me you'll still come to the wedding.'

'Of course I will,' Kari confirmed without hesitation. 'I wouldn't miss it for the world.'

'You're not angry with me for what I said?' Sarah probed cautiously, and Kari laughed softly.

'Sarah, you're my best friend. I know you said what you did because you care for me. It would take more than that to make me angry.'

'I simply want you to be as happy as I am.'

Kari knew that. Sarah was one of the few people who knew what had happened that summer day almost five years ago. Her support had been a great source of comfort to her.

'Seeing you happy makes me happy, goose. Now, I'd better get some work done before Jenny gives me one of her looks. Say hello to Mark when you see him.'

'OK. Oh, and one more thing. Will you join us for dinner on Thursday?' Sarah invited.

'I'd love to but I can't. Dad has invited a friend to dinner, and I promised I would be there. He's probably one of his old diplomatic cronies.' She had always called Russ's parents Mother and Dad, because her own parents had died when she was just a child.

'Sounds fun,' Sarah remarked drolly.

'I'll survive. Have fun, you two, and I'll call you in a couple of days.'

Kari set the receiver back down carefully and took several deep breaths. She would miss her friend when she was married. Their relationship would never be quite the same again. Mark would be the centre of her world, and so it should be.

Climbing to her feet, Kari went into the small washroom in the back to change into her work clothes. She paused, staring at herself in the mirror over the basin. Her reflection revealed a beautiful woman. Nothing showed of that dreadful act of violence over four years ago. Physically she was healed, but the invisible scars went deep.

Kari closed her eyes momentarily, then with a swift shake of her head reached for the work clothes she kept in a closet there. She had books to unpack, sort and catalogue. She wasn't going to think about the past any more today. She was going to bury herself in her work. She smiled grimly. That was the good thing about books. They couldn't hurt you. Not like life.

CHAPTER THREE

THE porch lights of the Maitland house glowed a welcome in the gathering dusk as Kari drove up the winding driveway on Thursday evening. Her headlights picked out a black sports car parked out front, and she pulled up behind it, frowning a little. So far as she was aware, only one guest had been invited tonight, and that impressively flashy car hardly seemed the type of vehicle an old friend of her father-in-law's would drive.

Inside the house she was greeted warmly by the Maitlands' long-time housekeeper, Lucy Drummond.

'It's good to see you again, Miss Kari,' she welcomed, taking Kari's jacket and draping it over her arm.

'You too, Lucy. I've missed your cooking. I hope you've prepared something special tonight.'

'That I have, Miss Kari, and they're all your favourites,' Lucy confided with a wink.

Kari's mouth began to water at the thought. Lucy's culinary expertise was to die for. 'Where is everyone?' she asked, glancing into the lounge and finding it empty.

'Miss Georgia hasn't come down yet, but you'll find Mr Robert in the library with his guest.' She rolled her eyes expressively as she turned away to hang up the coat.

Kari was left wondering what that was about, but as Lucy clearly had no intention of elaborating all she could do was shrug and head off in search of her father-in-law. The library was at the back of the house, a large, comfortable, book-lined room with a view over the gardens in daylight. As she approached the door she heard the clink of ice against glass, then the gurgle of liquid being poured. She smiled as she pictured her father-in-law pouring himself a glass of his finest malt whisky. It was his nightly ritual, and the continuity of it was comforting.

'Pour one for me while you're there,' she called out as she pushed open the door.

'Would that be with ice or water?' an unexpected, yet not wholly unfamiliar voice asked, and she came to an abrupt halt, staring at the figure who turned towards her, eyebrows raised enquiringly.

From his position by the credenza, Lance watched Kari frown, trying to place him. He had been expecting her since Robert had confirmed she was to be the other dinner guest. When he had heard her voice just now, a tingle of anticipation had raced across his skin, and he found himself watching her with undisguised pleasure.

She was everything he remembered, and more. He liked what he saw. Kari Maitland was a very elegant, extremely sensual woman. It was there in the way she walked and her choice of clothes. Tonight she wore a lacy black dress which stopped some way above her knees. Encased in sheer black nylon, her long legs were a man's fantasy come true, and once again he felt his body tighten in response to the thought of them wrapping around him as he made love to her. It was an effort to drag his gaze upwards, but he was rewarded for it. The slash neckline left her shoulders bare, revealing silky skin and the vulnerable curve of her nape. He had an urge to stroke it, to see if it would be as soft as he imagined.

His eyes came back to her face. She was still frowning. Any second now, the penny was going to drop, then he had better watch out for fireworks. If he knew one thing about Kari Maitland, it was that she was not going to be amused. But that didn't bother him. He liked her fire. He wanted to turn it into the passion he knew lay just beneath her cool façade.

Kari wasn't merely struggling with her memory. The instant he had turned, her whole system had been rocked by the powerful force which emanated from him. Her senses reacted instinctively, responding to the incredible potency of his maleness. He was quite staggeringly good looking. The sheer masculine beauty of him stirred her deeply, and her nerves skittered before she could get them under control, stealing her breath away. Who was he? There was something about him that…

It was his height which made the connection first, then the pull of his grey gaze. Those eyes! Her own widened as she recalled how it had felt to look into a pair just like them mere days ago, and how aware she had been of the man they belonged to. Just as now. In a microsecond she knew who he was, even though he looked totally different. Gone were the wrinkled jacket and disreputable whiskers. In an extremely expensive Italian suit and handmade shoes, with his hair combed and jaw shaven, he looked nothing like he had.

Her breath caught at the powerful surge of electricity which went through her. It was the second time he had done this to her, she thought incredulously. How did he do it? How on earth could he arouse her with no more than a look? It was…unnerving. He had no business coming here unsettling her this way!

Which served to remind her he had no business here at all. Outrage swelled inside her at the idea that he had invaded her in-laws' home. What underhand purpose was the snake about now? With a sharp intake of breath, she advanced on him.

'You! How dare you come here? What dirty trick are you trying to pull?' she demanded angrily, but didn't wait for him to respond. 'Whatever it is, let me tell you, you're not going to get away with it!'

'And it's a pleasure to see you again, too, princess,' Lance responded smoothly, biting back a grin and casually slipping one hand into the pocket of his trousers whilst he sipped at the drink he held in the other.

She hadn't let him down, and he almost laughed out loud, even though she was once more looking at him as if he had just crawled out from under a rock. She reminded him of a lioness rushing to the defence of her cubs. Kari Maitland was intensely protective of those she cared for. He liked that. He also very much liked the thought of doing battle with her again.

Kari caught the fleeting glint of amusement in his eyes and was sorely tempted to hit him. Only that would mean touching him, and instinctively she knew that that would be a bad move. If he could send her nerves haywire with a look, what could a touch do? No. She had to keep him at a distance, but even so she could make sure his pleasure at his perceived victory would be extremely short-lived.

'I think it's about time you left,' she suggested icily, and to her extreme aggravation the damned man merely smiled.

'But I've only just got here,' Lance argued reasonably, wondering to what lengths she would go to remove him. How would it feel to have her touch him? He just knew the touch of her hand would blow his mind.

Kari shot him a chilly smile. 'Good. That will make your visit short and sweet.'

No doubt that lethal look shot men down in droves, only it didn't work on him. It did the reverse. It made him want to see her melt in his arms.

'Don't you think your father-in-law ought to decide that?'

The fact that he was right only annoyed her more. Great, now he was teaching her good manners? She folded her arms determinedly. 'I have no idea what you told him to inveigle your way in here, but rest assured that once he knows the truth he will have you thrown out for the slime you are!' Kari returned acidly. She had no qualms about being deliberately rude. Maybe if she insulted him enough, he would leave of his own accord. She would rather not involve her father-in-law in a scene if she could help it.

Slime? Lance's smile deepened. She certainly was feisty. That tongue of hers had lost none of its edge. However, this time it wasn't going to get under his skin, however much she tried to rattle his cage. Besides, he had the advantage of knowing who he was, and he wasn't averse to stringing her along for a while longer.

'Are you sure?' he asked smoothly, and watched with interest as angry colour settled on her cheeks.

Goaded, Kari actually ground her teeth. 'My father-in-law knows scum when he sees it, even if it comes disguised in thousand-dollar suits.' Damn him, how many insults could he take before he had had enough and decided to leave? He had to have a hide like a rhinoceros and no sensitivity at all!

Scum? In the not too distant future he would make her pay for every single one of those insults—and he would guarantee they would both enjoy it. For now, he would satisfy himself with simply getting her to acknowledge her response to him. He knew instinctively she wouldn't like responding to the man she thought he was. It wasn't gentlemanly, but turnabout was fair play.

Lance strolled towards her, and saw her tense as he approached, her hands dropping to her sides as if ready to react. Oh, yes, the lady was very much aware of him. Though he was supposed to be arousing her, he could feel his own pulse racing. Closing the distance between them, he came to a halt a handful of inches away.

'Would you care to make a small wager on it?' he invited in a low, husky voice. He was rewarded by hearing her breath hitch, but at the same time had to stifle his own groan of masculine pleasure.

'What are you up to?' Kari demanded in a croak, and winced inwardly at the betraying sound. God, he was so close! Too close for comfort. Down by her sides, her hands balled into fists to stop herself from doing something silly—like reaching out to touch him. Which was a distinct possibility, the way he made her feel.

Her stomach had clenched on a powerful surge of desire as she watched him walk towards her with predatory, catlike grace. He had stopped close enough for her to be struck again by the sensual pull of his maleness, and her mouth had gone dry, her breath snagging in her throat. The air around them positively crackled with the electricity they generated. A person would have had to be made of stone not to feel it, and she was flesh and blood.

'Just getting you to put your money where your mouth is, princess.' Lance managed to shrug casually, although the betraying catch in her voice had made his own breathing go more than a little haywire.

Oh, yes, Kari Maitland was very much aware of him, and the knowledge aroused him swiftly. He had known he wanted her, but still he wasn't quite prepared for the strength of his own desire for her. Perhaps it was because his senses were no longer dulled by a hangover and lack of sleep that his response to this woman was almost...wild. He wanted her with an urgency that amazed him. There was something about her that aroused in him a primitive need to stake a claim to her. To make her his beyond any doubt. It was something he had never felt before, and he had to admit to being shaken by it.

Kari was feeling stunned too. He was standing so close, every breath she took brought with it the scent of him. His spicy aftershave teased her senses, whilst his distinct male fragrance was indescribably arousing. She was not proof against him, and as if to prove it her nipples started to harden in response to the sensual bombardment. She prayed he wouldn't notice.

'I don't gamble,' she rejected, determined not to sound as beleaguered as she felt, but then in the next instant her nerves skittered when he smiled. God, it was lethal. So was the glitter in his eyes. She drew in a ragged breath, an action which drew his eyes to her chest.

Lance saw the evidence of her arousal, and it shot his blood pressure skywards. Damn, he was acting more like a kid with raging hormones than a mature male. Maybe being this close had been a mistake. It did nothing for his self-control, which was suddenly dangerously rocky. He had to clear his throat in order to speak. Thinking clearly wasn't a piece of cake either.

'OK, we won't gamble for money. Let's say that if I win, you'll have dinner with me,' he suggested rather huskily. This close to her, he could smell her perfume and he had to fight the urge to close his eyes and just breathe her in.

Given her unbelievable susceptibility to the man, the very last thing Kari wanted to do was have dinner or any other meal with him. On the other hand, she hated backing down. How risky would it be to accept? She knew her father-in-law well, and his integrity. Because of it she knew this was a bet she could not lose.

'And if you lose?' she queried, looking up into eyes that seemed to draw her in. It took a determined effort to look away, and she licked her lips nervously, focusing instead on a spot somewhere near his left ear.

Lance saw her tongue peep out and had to suppress a groan. 'If I lose, you can have the personal satisfaction of throwing me out the door,' he returned with a careless shrug, because he knew it wasn't going to happen.

Kari would have felt elated but for the gleam in the eyes which watched her over his glass as he sipped at his drink. Her forehead creased into a frown. She couldn't help feeling she was missing something. Still, it hardly mattered, she comforted herself. He would be gone soon.

Until then it would be wise to put some much-needed room between them. If she stayed where she was, she had the uncomfortable feeling she would end up throwing herself at him just to ease the incredible tension surrounding them. Turning away, she crossed to the credenza and poured herself a mineral water. It annoyed her to find her hands were trembling faintly, and she took some deep breaths to steady herself. She could have done with something stronger, but her request for whisky had been a private joke. She drank very little, and never when she was driving.

Gathering her poise, she turned towards him, holding up her glass in a toast. 'To the victor.'

'The victor,' Lance acknowledged, doubting she realised how lovely she was with her chin tilted at that belligerent angle, daring him to do his worst. Their relationship was never going to be dull.

Silence fell between them, and Kari sought about for something to say to break it. She had never found it difficult to make small talk until now. Lord, his silence was as unsettling as his closeness had been, and his eyes never left her, not for a second. It made her feel fidgety, and she paced to the fireplace like a caged tigress.

'I...er...I take it that flashy sports car outside is yours?' she asked almost in desperation, and saw one eyebrow drift upwards.

'You disapprove?'

Kari produced an indifferent shrug, wanting him to know she wasn't impressed by him or his car. 'I'm sure it suits you down to the ground. All show and no substance.'

Lance winced at the double-barrelled shot. She sure knew how to deflate a man's ego. A man's car was an extension of himself. Belittle the car and you belittled him. Fortunately for him, the vehicle was a rental, and not one he would have chosen given a wider choice.

'Your opinion of me couldn't get any lower, could it?' he remarked, sitting down on the leather couch which faced the fireplace, angling himself so he could keep her in sight. He liked watching her move. She was as graceful as a gazelle, and just as easily spooked.

Kari regarded him narrowly. She didn't care for the way he sat down as if he expected to stay for hours. 'I wouldn't make myself too comfortable if I were you. The minute my father-in-law gets here, you're history. Where is he, by the way?' She had been so taken up with the unwelcome visitor, she had forgotten all about Robert.

'He went upstairs for something.'

Her eyebrows shot up. 'Leaving you here alone? You must have done some really smooth talking.' She didn't understand her father-in-law at all. As a rule he was a good judge of character. It just went to show how plausible this man was.

Lance knew exactly what she was thinking, and he grinned. She was going to go ballistic when she knew the truth. 'He trusts me,' he declared, and she smiled thinly.

'Not for very much longer. You could save yourself a lot of embarrassment by leaving of your own accord.' She, for one, would be delighted to see him go.

'Thanks for the concern, but I'll take my chances.'

Kari shrugged. 'Please yourself.'

'I generally do.'

He was so smug, Kari wanted to hit him, and she wasn't given to violence. She had seen more than enough of it to last her a lifetime. It was a relief to hear footsteps approaching down the hallway. Any second now this unpleasant business would be over and the damned man would be gone. Then she would do her level best to forget he even existed. A task, she suspected, which would be a great deal easier to say than to do.

Robert Maitland entered the room with his usual panache. He was a dapper man, slightly on the portly side, with a fine head of grey hair. His face broke into a smile when he saw his daughter-in-law. 'Kari, darling, I thought I heard you arrive,' he declared warmly, and held out his arms.

It was a revelation to Lance to see the way Kari Maitland's face changed when she turned to her father-in-law. Her smile and the look in her eyes showed a depth of affection that was entirely genuine. He found himself wanting her to look at him that way.

'Dad,' Kari murmured huskily as she returned his embrace.

'I see you've met Lance,' her father-in-law added brightly, turning so as to include the younger man.

'Oh, yes, I've met Lance all right,' Kari confirmed levelly, realising she hadn't actually known his name until that moment. Not that he would be here long enough for her to use it. 'I'm sorry to have to say this, Dad, but you've been misled. I have no idea what this man told you to get in here, but I advise you to have nothing to do with him. Not unless you want to see everything you say splashed across the front page of the tabloids tomorrow,' she added scornfully.

Robert Maitland couldn't have looked more dumbfounded. 'What on earth are you talking about, Kari?' her father-in-law charged in confusion.

'I think I can explain, Robert,' Lance interposed smoothly, getting to his feet. 'I'm afraid Kari is labouring under the misapprehension that I'm the editor of the *Examiner*,'' he enlightened his old friend.

Kari couldn't believe his gall. How could he think he could wheedle his way out of this when she was right there in front of him to prove his lie? 'You *are* the editor. I saw you with my own eyes. Or are you going to tell me it wasn't you I spoke to only a few days ago?' she countered immediately, her eyes daring him to deny that if he could.

'Oh, that was me all right,' Lance confirmed, unabashed. 'I happened to be using my cousin's office that day when you came in,' he added softly, and waited for the explosion. Because Kari Maitland was going to be furious.

It was Robert Maitland's turn to look mildly surprised. 'Fraser's your cousin?'

'For his sins,' Lance replied, not looking at Kari, but feeling the emotion boiling up inside her all the same.

'Oh, well, there's a rogue in every family.' Robert dismissed the connection easily, and turned to smile at Kari. 'It's Nick Fraser who edits the *Examiner*, darling,' he explained. 'Lance is what you might call a financial troubleshooter. He's the friend I told you I'd invited to dinner tonight.'

Speechless with rage, Kari's mouth opened and closed several times before she finally shut it with a loud clash of teeth. Her head snapped round and she glared at Lance, chest heaving with suppressed fury. How he must be laughing! Damn him! He had been playing games with her right from the very beginning! He had let her make a fool of herself for his own amusement. She would never forgive him for that. Never.

'I see,' she muttered through clenched teeth, barely holding onto her temper. 'How stupid of me.'

Lance met her eyes and winced inwardly. He was going to have to do some fancy footwork to soothe her ruffled feathers. 'It was a simple mistake to make.'

One he could have put right in a second, only he had chosen not to, Kari fumed silently. She would pay him back for it if it was the last thing she did.

Had they been alone, she would have given vent to her anger, but with Robert present she was forced to make light of it. 'You must have thought me a complete fool,' she responded with a stilted laugh, whilst sending Lance a withering look at the same time. He wasn't going to get away with this.

'Not at all,' he dismissed, fully aware it wouldn't wash with her. In retrospect, it really hadn't been a clever move not revealing who he was, but he couldn't do anything about it now.

Sublimely oblivious to the seething undercurrents, Robert urged Kari towards Lance. 'To avoid any further mistakes, I'd better introduce you properly,' he declared cheerfully. 'Kari, this is our friend Lance Kersee. Lance, meet Kari.'

Her father-in-law's presence made it impossible for Kari to refuse to shake hands with the man she was coming to loathe intensely. Her eyes glittered glacially, and it was with great reluctance that she held out her hand to him.

'I'm pleased to meet you, Mr Kersee,' she greeted evenly.

She was about as pleased as a Christian in a pit of hungry lions. Lance was very much aware that if she had had a knife, it would be hilt-deep in his back right now. He held her gaze for a second, a tiny smile hovering about his mouth. Then he reached across the gap separating them.

'I'm pleased to meet you, too, *Kari*,' he said point-edly as he took her hand.

They had never actually touched before this moment, and the effect was electrifying. A tingling warmth raced along her veins as her hand disappeared in his much larger one, and it stole her breath away. Tiny electric shocks set her nerve ends vibrating. Her eyes shot to his, and encountered the blazing depths of his grey eyes, reading the truth there. He was as aware of her as she was of him. Whatever she was feeling, he was feeling too. The attraction was mutual. He wanted her every bit as much as she wanted him.

'There now,' Robert Maitland declared in satisfaction. 'The formalities are out of the way and we can settle down to enjoying ourselves.'

The statement brought Kari back to her senses, and she pulled her hand away. Enjoy herself? She felt a bubble of hysteria lodge in her throat. It was unbelievable. This morning she had no notion of how the day would turn out. Now she found herself violently attracted to a man who thought nothing of lying, and who no doubt was laughing at her behind his back.

For once Kari did not enjoy an evening in the company of Russ's parents, though she was too well mannered to allow it to show for an instant. She laughed and chatted as if nothing were wrong, whilst all the time she was aware of Lance sitting opposite her, watching every move she made. It was hardly surprising that what appetite she had had fled, and she only picked at food she usually enjoyed.

She was so damned aware of him, her nerves screamed with it. Her stomach clenched every time she recalled how it had felt when they'd touched. How could a simple handshake do that? Irritated beyond words, she pushed her dessert plate away. She had gone years without feeling anything even resembling attraction, then Lance Kersee entered her life and she found herself lusting after him like the archetypal sex-starved widow.

Was that how he saw her? Her lip curled as she stared at him darkly. How could she doubt it? As soon as a man learned a woman was a widow, he assumed she must be starving for sex. Why should Lance be any different? No doubt he thought that, as she had revealed she was not unmoved by him, she would roll over at his command. Well, he was mistaken. She was not about to get to know him any better.

The evening dragged on interminably, and by half-past ten Kari had had enough. Usually she stayed chatting until almost midnight, but the presence of Lance Kersee made staying a minute longer impos-

sible to contemplate. He was deep in conversation
with Robert, and with any luck she hoped to slip
away without having to speak to him again.

'It's getting late. I must go,' she told Georgia
Maitland, who looked suitably regretful.

'Oh, must you, dear?'

Kari hated lying, but she simply had to leave. 'I'm
expecting an early delivery,' she invented as she got
up.

'Oh, well,' Georgia sighed, rising, then to Kari's
consternation she turned to her husband. 'Kari's leaving now, Robert,' she called out, unaware of her
daughter-in-law's intention of merely slipping away.

The two men glanced round at once, and both rose
to their feet.

'I'll walk you to your car,' Lance offered, and she
tensed in instant rejection. She had had quite enough
of his company already.

'That won't be necessary,' she refused with a tight
smile, but he just kept right on walking towards her,
taking her arm in a gentle yet firm grip.

'Bear with me. I had good manners instilled into
me as a child. A gentleman always sees a lady safely
to her car,' Lance countered smoothly, and Kari
seethed as she heard her in-laws agreeing with him.

Knowing it was impossible to reject the move
without appearing churlish, she was left no option
save to concur. Though she did mutter, 'You're no
gentleman,' under her breath, so that only he could
hear her.

His response was to utter a low laugh that skated
its way over her nerves, jangling them. 'Oh, but

you're wrong, Kari. Under the right circumstances, I can be a very gentle man,' he told her huskily, and hot colour seeped into her cheeks as she understood his meaning far too easily.

To her dismay, Kari had a clear vision of his hands stroking over her skin. The eroticism of it made her go hot all over. With a stifled sound she turned away from him, not wanting him to see her reaction, though she knew he would guess anyway. He seemed to know exactly how she would respond in any given situation.

'I'll get my coat,' she muttered thickly, and was intensely glad that he released her without comment.

She wasn't quite so pleased when he took her jacket from her, holding it out with a challenging glitter in his eye, and she could do nothing except accept his help. His hands lingered on her shoulders longer than she considered necessary, but as she opened her mouth to say so he removed them, leaving her trembling with anger that had nowhere to go.

Kari put on a smile as she bade her farewells to Russ's parents, then mentally girded herself to walk outside. Lance kept pace with her, their footsteps crunching on the gravel. The second they reached her car, she turned on him.

'Well, we're here. You've done your duty. You can go back now,' she informed him briskly, to which he responded with another of those slow smiles he did so well.

'In a second. We have something to discuss first.'

'I have nothing to discuss with you, Mr Kersee,' she denied as firmly as she could.

'Lance,' he corrected, and, at her swift icy glance of refusal, grinned. Another man might have been put off, but he saw it as encouraging. She could keep on fighting him for as long as she liked, but they both knew she was fighting herself as much as him. 'Scared to say it, princess?' he taunted, knowing she would rise to the bait.

She did, because there was no way she could show this man weakness. 'Lance.'

It was hardly music to his ears, but it would do for now. 'That wasn't so bad, was it?' he teased, and she shot him a withering look.

'Remind me to check up when I had my last tetanus shot,' she retorted frostily, and Lance laughed out loud.

'Kari, Kari, what am I going to do with that acerbic tongue of yours?'

His laugh did strange things to her insides, and she cursed her wilful senses which refused to obey the dictates of her brain. She didn't want to like anything about him. 'It's your own fault if you don't like what I say. Do you feel proud of the trick you pulled?'

Lance reached out to tuck a stray strand of her hair behind her ear, and she jumped as if she had been stung. 'As I recall, you were hardly sweetness and light yourself.'

His touch had sent shivers down her spine, and she instinctively took a half-step backwards. She had to keep some distance between them at all costs. 'I hope you don't expect me to apologise,' she declared sharply, and his laugh was wry as he followed her to close the gap again.

'Not in this lifetime, at any rate.'

Kari retreated again, and came up against the car. Unable to go any further, she was forced to stand her ground, but her heart picked up its pace. 'I'm glad you understand that. I wouldn't want to disappoint you.'

Having manoeuvred her into a corner, Lance decided not to press home his advantage and kiss her, even though he had an almost irresistible urge to taste her lips. He would find out how sweet they were another time. 'Oh, you won't disappoint me, princess. Far from it.'

Kari's breath caught in her throat at the husky remark. Damn it, why did he have to keep saying such outrageous things? Everything he said only contrived to make her more and more aware of him. They played tricks with her mind, turning her on when she wanted quite desperately to ignore him.

'For heaven's sake, will you stop calling me princess?' she ordered agitatedly.

'I have to call you something!'

'I do have a name!'

He smiled. 'I know, but princess suits you better.'

That did it! She decided she had had enough. 'I'm not standing around listening to any more of this,' she said unevenly, reaching into her bag for her car keys. She pulled them out and instantly dropped them. 'Damn it!'

'Take it easy,' Lance advised, bending to retrieve

the keys and holding them out to her. After a second or two, she reached over and took them from him.

'Thank you,' she said grudgingly.

'You're entirely welcome,' he returned smoothly, and she shot him an exasperated look.

'God, I hate you!' The revealing words were out before she could stop them, and she looked away in disgust.

Lance hid a smile. No, she didn't. She would like to, but she didn't. Ok, she didn't like him much right now, but she wanted him. The attraction was strong between them, and he would have to play a careful hand in order to win her round. He didn't doubt he could do it. It was going to take time, but he was a patient man. In the meantime, he couldn't resist teasing her.

'I knew you were a passionate woman from the moment I saw you,' he flirted, and Kari stared at him for a second, then shook her head angrily.

'Leave me alone, Lance,' she commanded scratchily.

'Now you know you don't mean that, princess,' he tutted.

Kari drew in a ragged breath. 'I do mean it.'

Lance smiled into her stormy eyes. He longed to see her rage turn to flames of passion and watch her blaze out of control. He wanted to know that he had been the one to make it happen, and then he wanted to be engulfed by it.

'No, you don't,' he countered softly. 'You want me as much as I want you.'

Hearing it put into words twisted her stomach into

knots. He made it sound so…settled. 'Do you usually get what you want?'

'Invariably,' he admitted, because it was true. He had a golden touch with business as well as with women.

She hated his confidence. It made her sound as if she were a pushover. If he thought that, he was mistaken. 'There's always an exception to the rule, and I'm it. I'm not available for your amusement.'

'We'll see.'

He made her so angry, she wanted to scream. 'Why won't you take no for an answer?' she charged frustratedly, and in answer he reached out and placed a finger on the pulse in her throat. It was already racing, but at his touch it shot off like a rocket.

'That's why,' he replied huskily, and knew he surprised her when he stepped back. 'Drive carefully, Kari. I wouldn't want anything to happen to you now.'

She blinked at him uncertainly for several seconds, then quickly climbed into the car before he could change his mind. She forced herself to manoeuvre the car carefully, not wanting him to think she was running away by shooting off down the drive. The last view she had of him was his tall dark figure silhouetted against the house as he looked after her.

As soon as she left the house behind, Kari pulled over to the side of the road. She was trembling. Damn, damn, damn. She didn't need this. Certainly didn't want it. Her fingers tightened around the steering wheel. He made her feel out of control, and she hated that. Yet he only had to come near her and her flesh tingled. A strangled laugh escaped her tight throat. He didn't even have to touch her!

She rested her forehead on the steering wheel and shivered. Deplore it though she might, she was immensely attracted to the man. He made her blood zing and her pulse race. Yet that didn't mean she had to fall into his arms, as he so arrogantly assumed she would. There was no way she was going to have an affair with him. She was more than a bundle of hormones. She had choices. She chose not to have anything to do with Lance Kersee.

The minute she decided that, she began to feel calmer. *She* had control of her life, not him. She didn't have to do anything she didn't want to. All she had to do was remember that. Bolstered, she put the car into gear and drove on. She was going to go home and get on with her life, and do her damnedest to forget she had ever met him.

CHAPTER FOUR

KARI swept a stray lock of hair off her face and shifted the ladder along to the next row of shelves. The shop was experiencing one of its rare moments of tranquillity, and she was taking advantage of it to put out some new stock. It also served a double purpose of keeping her out of the way until her mood improved.

She had not slept well, tossing and turning for ages, and then when she had drifted off into a restless sleep her dreams had all been about Lance Kersee. So much for forgetting all about him! She just might have been able to cope with the dreams, had they not been shockingly erotic to boot. Consequently she was in a touchy mood. She had already snapped Jenny's head off twice, and it was barely ten o'clock. In apology, she had sent her out to buy two of the gooiest cream cakes she could find, hoping that a large dose of sugar would sweeten her temper.

Working methodically, she had reduced the pile of new stock considerably and was on the top step of the ladder, sliding another couple of books into place, when she heard the bell ring as the shop door was opened.

'I won't keep you a moment,' she called out, balancing on tiptoe to reach a space above her head. She was either going to have to invest in a taller ladder or shorter shelving. It would have to be the former, for she could never contemplate reducing her stock. Perhaps she would get one that could circle the room on a rail, she mused idly.

Lance closed the door behind him and made his way towards her, enjoying the picture she made. She was dressed casually today. Leaning back against one of the stacks, he tipped his head on one side and took his time letting his eyes trace the shapely length of her legs. He liked the way the fabric of her jeans moulded her behind. It was neat and trim and just begged to be touched. Whichever way he looked at her, Kari was all woman. She didn't know it yet, but she was going to be his woman.

'Take your time. I'll just wait here and admire the view,' he drawled appreciatively.

With a sharp intake of breath, Kari swivelled her head round, her eyes widening as they met warm grey ones. Already poised in a precarious position, she was overbalanced instantly by the action. She teetered on the edge for a moment, arms windmilling crazily, then cried out as she felt herself falling.

Watching, Lance felt his heart give a sudden wild lurch as he saw her plummet towards the floor. Adrenaline surged, and he leapt forward, crossing the space between them in two quick strides, reaching out to catch her in his arms just in time. Holding her close, he closed his eyes and willed his heart to stop slamming against his chest. That had been too damn close.

It felt to Kari as if two steel bands closed around her, breaking her fall, then she was hauled in tight to something solid and warm. Her heart suddenly caught up with her, racing like a train, and in her ear she could hear another beating in time. She opened her eyes to find Lance's anxious face hovering mere inches above hers.

'I knew you'd fall into my arms one day, princess,' he joked, but his voice sounded ropy even to his own ears.

She'd given him one hell of a fright there. Damn it, Kersee, he remonstrated himself, she could have broken her neck, and it would have been your fault. The very real possibility was sobering. She continued to stare up at him with eyes like blue pools a man could easily drown in, and with a faint groan he gave in to the temptation which had been riding him for days now, and kissed her.

Kari had been so struck by the terror on his face that she quite forgot to move when she saw his head lower. Then, of course, it was too late. Her system closed down at the first touch of his mouth on hers, and she promptly forgot to breathe. His lips were warm and gentle, and oh, so sure. Her own tingled in response as he brushed them. He used barely any pressure at all, and made no attempt to deepen the kiss, but she felt him to the tips of her toes. Her eyelids fluttered, suddenly growing too heavy to stay open. She sighed, and of its own accord her free hand slipped up to cradle the back of his neck, starting a slow caress that matched the steady brush of his lips on hers.

Her soft touch sent flames shooting through him like wildfire, and with a low growl Lance parted her

lips with his tongue and plunged inside. She tasted
like nectar, hot and sweet, and it made him a little
giddy. When he felt her tongue flick against his, the
world went spinning crazily away. In an instant he
was plundering her mouth as if he couldn't get
enough of her.

Kari met his hungry kisses with a hunger of her
own. Each stroke of his tongue had her moaning achingly and searching for more. Her whole body felt
incredibly alive, and she pressed herself against him
with simmering urgency, wanting the magic to go on
and on. She wanted...

The harsh jangle of the doorbell brought her eyes
open in alarm, bringing her also to the stark realis-
ation of where she was and exactly what she was
doing. Panting as if she had just run a gruelling race,
she stared up at Lance incredulously, hot colour in-
vading her cheeks as she recalled her response. Dear
God, what was she thinking of? She had to be out
of her mind! Damn, damn, damn, she groaned silently, thrusting her hands against his shoulders.

Lance only slowly caught on to what was happening. The second his lips had touched hers, he had
stopped thinking. He'd forgotten where he was, and
that had never happened to him before. Some part of
his mind had always remained detached, no matter
how involved he'd been, but not with this woman.
He had always known she was different, but he was
only now beginning to realise just how much. She
had the ability to drive everything from his mind,
except the incredible wonder of making love to her.

Then he felt her struggling to break free, and blinked down at her.

'Put me down!' she hissed, hearing the sound of humming which told her it was Jenny returning. She did not want to be found in a compromising position with this man.

'Say please,' he couldn't resist teasing in a sensually husky voice, and, hearing the footsteps getting closer, Kari could do nothing more than glare at him and capitulate.

'Please!' she snapped under her breath, and found herself standing upright again, her feet planted firmly on the ground. An instant later Jenny came into view.

'Sorry I took so long, Kari, but—oh!' She stopped midsentence when she saw her employer was not alone.

Kari watched her assistant look Lance up and down with feminine appreciation, and wanted to slap her. The jealous response appalled her. Good God, what was the matter with her? She absolutely had no intention of claiming him as her property. Then Jenny actually smiled at him with a certain look in her eye, and Kari felt her stomach tighten. She had the sudden urge to step between them and warn her assistant off. This was ridiculous. She didn't want him. She didn't!

Lance picked up Kari's tension and glanced at her out of the corner of his eye. He was amused and secretly delighted by the faintly hostile expression she wore. He liked the idea that the lady was jealous. 'Aren't you going to introduce me?' he prompted.

She didn't want to, and she preferred not to ask

herself why. 'This is Jenny, my assistant,' she said curtly.

'Lance Kersee.' Lance held out his hand. 'Pleased to meet you, Jenny.'

'Likewise,' Jenny responded, almost simpering to Kari's disgust.

Seeing the emotion flash briefly across her expressive face, Lance smothered a grin. 'I won't keep Kari long. I only came to remind her about our date tonight.'

'Date?' Kari and Jenny echoed, in varying degrees of surprise.

'What date?' Kari added tensely.

Lance slipped his hands into his trouser pockets and quirked an eyebrow at her. 'You haven't forgotten we're having dinner?' he remonstrated softly, reminding her of their bet the previous night.

Kari's mouth opened but no words came out. She had forgotten, but even if she hadn't her response would have been the same. She had no intention of having dinner with him, nor of arguing the point in front of others. She glanced meaningfully at Jenny who was now watching the pair of them with undisguised interest. Oh, great, the last thing she needed was the rumour mill to start grinding!

Jenny got the message. 'I'd better go and put these in the refrigerator,' she declared prudently, indicating the bag she held, and, smiling vaguely at neither, made herself scarce.

The instant they were alone, Kari turned on him. 'You can't possibly think for one second that I'd have dinner with you!' she exclaimed forthrightly.

'Welching on the bet, princess?' Lance asked goadingly, and her eyes shot daggers at him.

'The dice were loaded in your favour and you know it! There's no disgrace in refusing to honour it,' she told him, and dared him to argue with that.

He didn't even try. 'Coward,' he accused softly, and, as he had known she would, Kari balked at the word.

'I am not a coward,' she denied, and Lance pressed home his advantage remorselessly.

'Admit it. You're afraid of me.'

Her laugh was scoffing. 'That'll be the day!'

'Liar,' he countered, making her gasp angrily. 'You're afraid I might win.'

A shiver chased its way along her spine. 'Win what, precisely?' she asked, though she was pretty sure she knew. He wanted her to have an affair with him, and she was damned if she was going to do it. Not after the way he had behaved.

'The battle.'

'There is no battle,' she declared with a lift of her chin, and he smiled right into her eyes.

'If that's the case, princess, then there's no reason for you not to have dinner with me, is there?' he contested succinctly.

Kari's eyes narrowed as she realised how neatly he had trapped her. She had foolishly forgotten how smart he was, how devious. He had used her against herself. Now she was caught because her pride would not allow her to refuse the challenge.

'I'm surprised someone didn't murder you years

ago,' she remarked acidly, and he had the gall to laugh.

'You won't think that when you know me better.'

Kari gave an unladylike snort. 'I know you as well as I intend to. I'll have dinner with you, but that's all there will ever be between us.'

Lance admired the way she continually fought him; it kept him on his toes. 'That wasn't the impression I got just now,' he reminded her unnecessarily.

Kari crossed her arms and smiled sweetly. 'Impressions can be deceptive. I wouldn't put too much faith in them if I were you.'

'I could prove you wrong right now, but unfortunately I don't have the time.'

Shooting back his cuff, he glanced at the gold Rolex on his wrist. He had a meeting to attend, and he was going to be cutting it fine. He hadn't intended to stay above a couple of days, but meeting Kari had forced him to change his plans. Contacting his office, he had had his secretary rearrange schedules. It hadn't been easy, but he had arranged for his deputy to do some exploratory work in Denver, whilst he took on a project here on the east coast. That was what this meeting was all about.

'I've got to go. I'll pick you up at seven-thirty. Don't be late.' He reached out and ran a finger gently down her cheek. 'By the way, I'm glad you're jealous, princess, but there's no need for you to be. The only woman I'm interested in is you,' he declared huskily before heading for the door. There he paused momentarily and looked back at her over his shoulder. 'Oh, and wear something sexy,' he commanded, and the memory of the way her eyes flashed went with him out the door.

Kari stared at the closed door and fumed impotently. She was not jealous. Jenny was welcome to him. Any and all women were welcome to him! As for that last remark—wear something sexy? She would do no such thing. If she had anything approaching sackcloth, she would wear it. She did not want to encourage him—not that he needed encouragement. Lance Kersee was a law unto himself, a man used to getting his own way. Well, he was mistaken if he thought she would simply fall into his arms. The man might not be who she thought he was, but he had played her for a fool, and she hadn't forgiven him for it. She was not going to be his next bedmate.

Which was all very well and good to say, but she would prefer it if her lips didn't still tingle from the touch of his, reminding her constantly of how mind-blowing his kisses were. Damn it, she thought crossly, she had to make sure he did not catch her off guard again. Her defences would never withstand too many of his kisses. Just thinking about them now made her go weak at the knees! Abruptly deciding her legs were too shaky to attempt climbing, Kari put the ladder away in its corner and returned to the office.

Jenny had made coffee, and she offered Kari a mug. 'He's nice,' she remarked casually.

'Who?' Kari pretended ignorance. She did not

want to talk about Lance. Thinking about him was quite enough.

Jenny laughed. 'Right, who?' she scoffed and Kari's cheeks turned pink.

Nice was not the word she would choose to describe Lance. Objectionable, loathsome, devious…sexy, exciting and drop-dead gorgeous. Stop it, she commanded with a silent groan. Enough!

'Don't read anything into it. Lance's a friend of my father-in-law.'

'Maybe he is, but he wants to be more than friends with you,' Jenny observed dryly.

If there was one thing Kari did not need to be told, that was it. 'Then he's going to be disappointed,' she declared with determination.

'I thought you liked him,' her assistant responded in confusion, and Kari gave her a wary look.

'Whatever gave you that idea?' she asked, striving to be nonchalant.

Jenny pretended to think about it. 'Let me see…I think it was when you looked as if you wanted to kill me for smiling at him,' she said wryly, and the pink in Kari's cheeks deepened to a fiery glow.

'I…I…couldn't have done anything so rude,' she gasped faintly, but knew she had. It was Lance's fault. Ever since he had entered her life, she had been behaving out of character.

'Don't worry about it.' Jenny dismissed it with a shrug. 'I'm a woman, too. I understand these things. I'm happy for you, Kari. I never thought I'd see you with a real man. Boy, was he real!' she finished with a grin.

Kari smiled weakly. She certainly couldn't argue with that. There was an energy about Lance which set her nerves tingling. He made her feel things that made her shiver just remembering them.

'I think I'd prefer to change the subject,' she said abruptly, not wanting to think about Lance any more right now.

'OK,' Jenny conceded accommodatingly. 'Actually I meant to ask you if you'd read the papers this morning, because there's something in the *Examiner* you aren't going to believe.'

'I tend not to believe *anything* I read in that rag,' Kari returned caustically.

Her assistant laughed, and sorted through a pile of newspapers for the one she wanted, then began searching through the pages. 'I know what you mean, but that isn't what I meant. It's tucked inside, but it's there.'

'What is?' Kari asked curiously.

Jenny found the page she wanted and folded it open. 'An apology,' she declared, handing the paper over and pointing to a small paragraph at the bottom.

Bending over, Kari read it, then read it twice more, her chin dropping. 'I don't believe it!' she gasped.

'I couldn't believe my eyes either,' her assistant agreed.

Kari didn't hear her, she was too busy taking in the fact that before her eyes was the apology she had demanded just the other day. It was small and hidden away, but it was there. Totally dumbfounding her, because she hadn't spoken to the editor at all, only Lance. Lance! She closed her eyes helplessly, knowing that that could mean only one thing. Her words had not fallen on deaf ears. Lance must have read the article and somehow persuaded his cousin to print the apology.

She winced, but at the same time a tiny glow of warmth started up inside her at what he had done. The man she had reviled had gone in to bat for her—and won. That changed everything. How could she despise him after this? OK, his reasons for helping her might have been self-serving, no doubt designed to aid him in his intention of getting her into bed, but the result was the same. The apology had been printed, and she was going to have to thank him. It would be unjust to do anything less.

Mind you, that didn't excuse him for playing that rotten trick on her, even if he had apologised for it. She wasn't going to forgive him that easily. So he needn't think she was going to fall into his arms like a ripe plum, however irresistible he was. He might have proved he was not the loathsome man she had thought him, but it altered nothing. He was too darn sure of her capitulation, but he was about to find out he wasn't going to get her that easily. Oh, no. She had her pride. She would fight him tooth and nail.

Which perversely confirmed she was locked in the battle she had just told him did not exist. A battle where he was going to do his best to get her into bed, and she was going to have to play it very cool indeed to keep out of it for as long as possible. Her nerves jolted. As long as possible! That seemed to suggest she knew she was going to end up in his bed sooner or later. Was she crazy? Quite possibly, but the prospect of being made love to by the man brought her out in goose-bumps.

The truth was, whatever she said, she wanted him. She had to be honest with herself at least. It was no longer a matter of if, but when. It didn't matter that she'd only known him a few days. The attraction was powerful, and she wanted to explore it. But as she had already said, she was not about to offer herself to him on a plate. She was going to hold out as long as she could, to put him in his place. Which meant at the very least she had to make sure she did not end up in his arms again. She was too susceptible when he touched her.

They would have dinner as planned, and some time during the evening she would thank him for his help in getting the apology printed. That was all, absolutely all, that would happen.

That was her plan, but it didn't quite turn out that way.

It started to go wrong when Kari opened the door to Lance at seven-thirty that evening. Outwardly she gave no sign of what happened, but inwardly... The impact of the mere sight of him was incredible. He made her legs go weak at the knees. Her thought processes ground to a halt, even as her pulse-rate increased. Then he smiled, completing the mayhem, and she knew she was in trouble. She was fighting a losing battle. Her will had no control over her senses, they kept on responding to the signals he sent out, and the result was electrifying. Every atom of her was pleased to see him. Her stomach kicked, and she pressed a faintly trembling hand against it.

It was all she could do to keep her voice steady. 'I won't be a second, I just have to get my bag,' she told him, relieved to hear she still sounded calm, and hoping he would stay where he was and give her time to recover. She should have known better. He followed her inside.

She wasn't as calm as she would have him believe, Lance thought. He wondered how much effort it was taking for her to appear cool and detached. Quite a lot, if his own response was anything to go by. He didn't think he would ever get to the stage where setting eyes on her didn't set his pulse racing.

She was wearing what she considered was the least sexy item in her wardrobe. It brought a smile to his lips. One day he was going to tell her she would look sexy in a sack. This dress, made of some silky blue material, covered her from her neck to a little above her knees, and had long sleeves to boot. However, as he followed her inside, it moved against her in such a way as she walked that it showed off every feminine curve of her body.

His own reacted immediately, but he was getting used to that now. Her perfume wafted behind her, a delicate fragrance that teased his nostrils and made him want to breathe her in.

'Nice room,' he commented as they entered the living room, glancing round appreciatively.

It reverberated warmth and comfort, and told him more about her than she probably suspected. She was a born home-maker. It showed in her choice of throws and cushions, even the rug they walked on. This was a room where children could play without fear of breakage, and in which a man could take his shoes off and put his feet up. It was a place he would be eager to get back to—providing she was here.

Kari picked up her bag from where she had left it on the arm of a chair, took a deep steadying breath and turned to face him. 'OK, I'm ready,' she announced.

'There's just one thing before we go,' Lance declared, circumventing her intention to walk past him to the door.

She frowned in consternation. She didn't want him to linger here. She did not want to be able to picture him in her home. She didn't need that kind of sensory torture. The man was unforgettable enough as it was. 'What is it?'

'Just this,' he said, closing the few feet separating them. Catching her chin between finger and thumb, he tilted it a fraction and brought his mouth down on hers.

Kari was too startled to prevent it, then too mesmerised to move away. His lips claimed hers in a leisurely fashion, teasing her, then his tongue stroked along her full bottom lip and the sensation stole her breath away. She gasped and shivered, expecting more, needing more, but in the next second he was moving back and, to her dismay, for one tiny instant she swayed towards him as if to prolong the contact. It was intensely revealing to both of them.

'I've been waiting to do that since this morning,' he declared seductively. 'I wanted to know if your kiss would be as sweet as I remembered. Kari, honey,

I do believe I could become addicted to the taste of your lips.'

He had done it again, the unprincipled rogue! Heat washed into her cheeks as she struggled to regain her poise. 'I doubt you'll be getting the opportunity,' she countered repressively. So much for not letting him take her by surprise.

'I hope you're not about to tell me you didn't enjoy it too?' Lance remarked softly. 'I didn't take you for a liar.'

Her eyes flashed at that. 'And you should know, if anyone does!'

Lance inclined his head in acknowledgement. 'I guess I asked for that,' he returned with a rueful smile. 'How long is it going to take to get you to forgive me?'

Kari sent him a withering look, accompanied by a less than friendly smile. 'How does for ever sound?' she suggested tartly.

He laughed delightedly. It was an old cliché, but she was magnificent when she got mad. 'How about if I grovel?'

She tipped her head to one side consideringly. 'The idea does have a certain piquant charm. How good are you at it?'

'You'd make me do it, wouldn't you?' he charged, grinning.

'Can you give me one good reason why I shouldn't?' Kari knew she shouldn't be encouraging him this way, but, darn it, she was beginning to actually enjoy these exchanges. They were almost as tantalising as his kisses.

Lance rubbed his nose thoughtfully before looking at her quizzically. 'Because deep down inside you really like me?' he proposed with a boyish grin, whilst inside he held his breath. The question wasn't as innocent as it seemed. He needed to know if he was making up some of the lost ground.

Kari's stomach lurched. Did she like him? Now that she had actively stopped disliking him, the truth was obvious. She liked him too much for her own good. Still, she wasn't about to tell him. Couldn't afford to, considering her intention of keeping him at bay for as long as she could.

'I'd say that's for me to know and you to find out,' she retorted smartly, and her heart promptly kicked when his alluring smile appeared.

'You like me,' he declared confidently, rocking back on his heels, and she frowned at him fiercely.

'I never said that,' she argued, but he shook his head.

'If you still disliked me, you would have said so, to my face. *Ergo*, you like me.'

'God, you are so aggravating!' she exclaimed in exasperation, because it was true. She would have had no qualms about admitting her dislike. She wasn't sure she liked the fact that he knew it.

'I'll grow on you,' he rejoined, and it was all she could do to stop herself from stamping her foot. Something only he seemed capable of making her do.

'Could we please just go now?' she asked in a long-suffering tone.

Lance stepped back with a smile. 'Your wish is my command, princess.'

She walked past him with her head tilted at an imperious angle, which would have been worthy of a real princess.

He drove into Portland, to a restaurant situated on the top floor of a new and very exclusive hotel. Every table was set just far enough away from the others to allow for privacy, and the lighting was way down low. Her heart did a little skip when she walked in. She could have wished for something less intimate, but nevertheless the ambience was subtly relaxing. They were shown to a table by the window which offered a spectacular view out over the city. The sun was going down, and soon lights would begin coming on, turning the everyday world into a more magical place.

'What would you like to drink?' Lance asked, and because she wasn't driving she chose a glass of white wine. Lance added his own preference and the waiter disappeared, leaving them alone.

Kari looked around her with interest, finding herself nodding to several acquaintances she knew through her in-laws. 'I had no idea this place existed,' she confided honestly, turning to her companion. 'How on earth did you find it?'

'It wasn't too difficult. One of my uncles owns the hotel,' Lance admitted dryly. 'My family's business interests are as diverse as the members of it.'

Kari nodded wisely. 'Ah, that would explain it.'

Lance's eyebrow curved upwards. 'Explain what?'

he asked, enjoying watching the way her lips quirked in silent amusement. It made him want to smile too.

She looked at him mockingly. 'How you managed to procure such a prime spot by the window.'

He shrugged, refusing to feel guilty. 'They reserve it for family or special guests.'

'Of course. My, how the other half live!' she exclaimed ironically.

'Tut-tut, your prejudices are showing,' Lance responded with a lazy grin. 'Besides, are you trying to tell me you don't snap up the books you fancy before they get to the shelves?' he challenged.

Touché. 'Of course not. It's one of the perks of the trade.'

Lance spread his hands. 'My point exactly. You get the books, I get the table by the window.' Their drinks arrived, and Lance took a mouthful of his before continuing. 'But let's not argue. Tell me what you think of the view.'

For once she was happy to fall in with his wishes. She didn't want to argue either. 'It's marvellous,' she admitted honestly.

'Good. I thought you'd appreciate it.'

She took a sip of her wine, delighting in the burst of flavour on her tongue. 'You did?'

'Oh, yes. You're a very classy lady. I could see from your home you have exquisite taste,' he said smoothly, and she couldn't help smiling faintly at the compliment.

'Are you trying to charm me, by any chance?'

'Is it working?' he asked, and she knew she wouldn't dare admit that it was. She couldn't afford to be charmed by him too easily if she wanted to stay out of his bed.

'I saw the apology in the paper today,' she remarked, unabashedly changing the subject. 'I was surprised.' What an understatement!

Lance laughed softly, reading into the change what she would not admit. He could afford to let it pass. 'I bet you were even more surprised when you realised I must have had a hand in it,' he retorted sardonically, and she flushed.

'You can hardly expect me to have anticipated it after...' She shrugged, not quite knowing how to refer to their first encounter politically.

His grin deepened. 'After you chewed me out, you mean.'

'I wouldn't have put it quite like that.' She winced.

'There's no need to feel embarrassed. You did it very well. In fact, nobody has done it better, not even my sister, and she knows how to cut a man down to size,' Lance revealed drolly.

Kari wondered what his sister was like. She liked the sound of her. Clearly she didn't allow him to get away with anything, and, equally clearly, he didn't mind being ordered around by her. They must love each other very much. Being an only child, and then orphaned, she had no idea what that kind of relationship was like. She had always wanted brothers and sisters, and had been determined that she would have more than one child. But that was in the past. Her priorities had changed.

She pulled her thoughts back on line before they

travelled too far down that road. 'Anyway, I realise it must have been awkward for you.'

'Not at all.' Lance denied the notion with a wave of his hand. 'I don't happen to approve of my cousin's job, and he knows it. I'm trying to persuade him to take his talents to where they could do more good. As he printed the apology, I've a feeling I'm beginning to wear him down,' he told her honestly, leaving her once more at a loss.

He was turning out to be very different from what she had expected, and the less obnoxious he became, the more she needed to make amends. 'Nevertheless, I should still thank you for your help.'

In response, Lance picked up a menu and handed it to her. 'You just have, now why don't we forget about it?' he suggested, but Kari shook her head swiftly. Fair was fair.

'I have to make amends for being so rude to you, too,' she added, and, seeing that she was determined, Lance sighed.

'How do you propose to do that?'

Kari frowned. 'By apologising, of course.'

He was about to accept it when a devilish idea occurred to him, and he resisted it for all of ten seconds. Why take an apology when he could get more? All was fair in love and war. 'Sorry, princess, but actions speak louder than words.'

She wasn't sure she liked the sound of that. 'What do you mean?'

'I was thinking along the lines of some sort of penance,' he said thoughtfully. 'Nothing too difficult.

I'll have to think about it. I'm sure I can come up with something.'

'I'm sure you will,' Kari agreed dryly, taking the menu from him. 'Why do I get the feeling you aren't to be trusted?'

Lance smiled faintly. 'Because you have a suspicious mind?' he murmured, turning his attention to his own menu, secure in the knowledge that she would be in his arms again before the night was out, by fair means or foul.

Kari stared at his down-bent head. Too right she was suspicious. A wise woman would keep her wits about her, and she planned to be very wise indeed.

CHAPTER FIVE

MUCH later, lingering over coffee, Kari somewhat reluctantly acknowledged that she had enjoyed herself. The food had been every bit as good as she'd imagined it would be, whilst her companion had been witty and serious by turns, and effortlessly charming. She felt at ease with him, probably because he had gone out of his way to make her so. That vibrant awareness was still present, but it had slipped into the background where it remained leashed but untamed. She had no doubt it would flare up at the slightest opportunity, but she felt too relaxed and mellow to worry about it right now.

Setting her cup down, she turned her attention to the view outside. She liked the city best at night, when you couldn't see the dirt and the meanness of everyday life. They were very high up, but that didn't bother her. Russ couldn't have sat here and enjoyed it with her, though—he had always hated heights. The memory made her sigh a little wistfully.

Across the table, Lance studied her profile, his eyes caressing every curve. She was an achingly beautiful woman, and he felt his heart expand as he watched her. Love was a pretty powerful emotion, and he loved this woman so much, he would gladly die for her. Though he hoped it wouldn't come to that. He would much prefer living with her.

She shifted slightly so the light caught her, throwing shadows, and he frowned. There was something fragile about her. He sensed rather than saw a deep sadness in her at that moment, and her soft sigh was full of regret. His throat closed over, something twisting painfully inside him at the sound.

'What were you thinking?' he asked, instinctively speaking softly.

Kari started at the sound of his voice. She had been light years away. Now she half turned towards him, shaking her head. It didn't seem right to admit she was thinking of another man when she was here with him, even though they were nothing to each other. 'You wouldn't be interested.'

He found he was as possessive as the next man, and couldn't help wondering what it was she didn't want him to know. 'Try me. I may surprise you,' he insisted in the same gentle tone, and she turned to face him squarely.

His persistence surprised her. Why would a man whose main aim in life was getting her into bed be interested in her thoughts? It didn't make a lot of sense. However, if he wanted to know, she had no hang-up about telling him.

'I was remembering that Russ had no head for heights,' she told him, whilst the fingers of her right hand unconsciously twisted her wedding band.

Lance's eyes followed the movement, and, though he had a pretty good idea whom she was referring to, he still sought clarification. 'Russ?'

She glanced down at her hands briefly. 'Russ is...*was*, my husband,' she corrected herself.

Lance went utterly still as something unexpected occurred to him. He had quite forgotten she was a widow. The fact posed a problem he hadn't considered. Was she still in love with her late husband? He realised that, in his pursuit of her, he had never given much thought to the possibility. It was entirely possible, and if true what hope was there for him? He felt the sands shift dangerously under his feet. How the hell did he fight the memory of a dead man? He had no idea, but first he had to find out if it was something he had to deal with seriously.

Reaching across the table, he took her hand in his, raising her fingers and running his thumb over the diamond-studded ring.

'You still miss him?' he asked as casually as he could, and his blood chilled when he felt her instinctive retreat.

This was ground she rarely ventured onto because of the painful memories. 'Of course. He was my husband. I loved him,' Kari returned sharper than she intended, and tugged her hand free.

Lance sat back, eyeing her watchfully. It had been a stupid question, and he was no better off for the answer. She might have said 'loved', the past tense, but the connection was still strong. The man who won Kari Maitland would have to accept that a part of her heart would always belong to her first husband.

He knew he would never begrudge her that. She was the woman she was because of her marriage to Russ Maitland. It was that woman he had fallen in love with. But he was only human, and he was curious. If he wanted to know what made Kari tick, he had to know more about her late husband.

'How long is it since he died?'

'Five years.' Give or take a week or two. It had been summer, like now. One of those long sultry days. It had seemed like heaven; it had turned into hell. She had lost more than Russ that day. She hadn't been near a stable since. Her beloved horses had been sold, for she had been unable to find solace with them. They made her remember, and remembering hurt too much.

'What happened to him? How did he die?' he asked automatically, and even though he was no longer touching her he felt the tension which ripped through her. His mind jolted. What the hell had happened to Russ Maitland?

Kari drew in a painful breath as broken images raced through her mind. She didn't want to tell him anything, but the events of that day were a matter of public record. If she said nothing, she knew he was quite capable of finding out on his own, and there were details she preferred to keep private. It would be better to give him a watered-down version and hope he would be satisfied with that.

'He was shot,' she said tightly. Russ had died in her arms before help could arrive. He had literally bled to death, and she hadn't been able to do anything to save him.

Never in a million years would Lance have expected her to say that. He had been thinking of some sort of accident, but this was something else. He felt her pain like a tangible thing, and it was as if an invisible fist had slammed into his chest.

'Hell, princess, I'm sorry,' he declared gruffly.

Kari's breath caught at the look in his eyes. The compassion there was stunning. It was almost as if he knew exactly what she had gone through. Yet he couldn't possibly know what it had been like for her. He hadn't been there. How could he look at her as if he felt the pain too? Her heart contracted, then raced frantically. He scared her with his insight. She didn't like the idea that he could see so much. Didn't want him to know her, and understand her, and get so close.

Her chin lifted proudly. 'I don't need your pity.'

He knew what she was doing was a purely reflex action, but it hurt all the same. 'Hell, princess, don't be so polite. Give it to me right between the eyes,' he retorted with an edge.

Kari winced, knowing she had been unfair. 'I'm sorry. I know you meant well.' It was simply that he had seen more than she expected. It had put her off balance for a moment.

'Do you reject everyone this way, or is it just me?' he asked, striving for a milder tone.

Kari suspected her answer to that wouldn't please him either, but she said it anyway. 'You're not special enough to be treated differently,' she told him, and to her amazement he began to smile.

'I'm glad to hear it,' Lance retorted wryly. She had a million ways to put a man down, and he had the feeling he was going to learn them all before they were through.

Kari was perplexed. How did he do that? Laugh when she expected anger? She'd never understand him, not if she lived to be a hundred. Not that she wanted to understand him. She didn't. He was so…frustrating.

'Did they ever catch the person who did it?' Lance asked, and saw something cold and deadly enter her eyes at the question. It shocked him to recognise pure hatred.

'No. He vanished off the face of the earth. But I'd know him if I ever saw him again,' she said chillingly. His face was as clear in her mind now as it had been five years ago. One day he would pay, as his partner had paid for his part in the events which had unfolded.

'You were there?' Lance asked in surprise. He hadn't expected that. How many more shocks would she give him?

'Oh, yes. I was there,' she confirmed grimly.

Lance felt his stomach clench. There was a wealth of things unspoken in those few words, and he found himself wondering once again what she wasn't telling him. His heart lurched sickeningly. God, what else had happened? He wanted to demand answers, but he knew, as certainly as he knew his own name, that if he asked she would not tell him. He would have to let it go—for now.

'That must have been rough,' he managed to say in a nearly normal voice.

Kari's lips twitched. That was putting it mildly. 'I've had better days,' she remarked ironically and lost her breath at the rage which suddenly flared in his eyes.

'Don't be so damned flippant!' Lance ordered in an explosive undertone, and Kari stared at him dumbly. What was he getting so angry about? It had happened to her, not him.

Lance answered her unspoken question. 'You could have been killed too.' The thought of it sent a chill down to the depths of his soul.

Kari swallowed to clear a painfully tight throat. 'I'm sorry. I didn't think you would want to hear the truth,' she apologised, hardly believing she was doing it. Suddenly she was in the wrong. How had he done it?

Lance's eyes narrowed on her compellingly. 'I want nothing but the truth from you, Kari. Ever,' he declared forcefully, holding her gaze.

Her heart thudded anxiously, and she eyed him warily. 'All right. You want the truth. The truth is it was hell. It was the worst day of my life, bar none. Is that what you wanted to hear?'

Lance felt the anger seep out of him. He had always prided himself on his control, yet he had almost lost it when she'd tried to make light of what had happened. Dying was no laughing matter. He might have lost her before he'd ever found her!

They stared at each other across the table, and it was Lance who broke the silence. 'I'm sorry.'

Her eyebrows rose. Was that it? He had just scared the living daylights out of her and that was all he had to say? It wasn't nearly enough. 'Sorry for what, precisely?' she asked, and received one of those nerve-tingling, lopsided smiles for her pains. Right on cue her toes curled.

'I'm sorry I blew my top. My only defence is that I was expecting to hear you say your husband died in an accident,' Lance declared wryly.

Kari found she could accept that. She would so much rather have been able to tell him Russ had died in a road accident. Had it been true, it would have been tragic enough. The truth was another country, and it had broken her heart—because, guiltless as she was, his death had still been her fault. If only she hadn't gone to the stable that day... No. She gave herself a mental shake. She wasn't going to do that to herself. 'If only's' were pointless, they didn't change anything. Russ was still dead; she was still alone.

'You've never been married, have you, Lance?'

He quirked one eyebrow lazily. 'How do you know I'm not?'

Her heart skipped a beat. She had never considered the possibility, had simply assumed that as he was pursuing her he wasn't, which was rather naive.

'Are you?'

'Would it bother you if I was?' he teased.

'Of course it would. I don't date married men,' she shot back frostily, then closed her eyes when she realised what she had said.

'So, this is officially a date, is it?' he queried with a grin, and her breath came out in an irritated puff.

'Do you enjoy playing games?'

'Only with ladies with sad eyes,' he countered silkily, and her nerves leapt.

Kari disliked being so easy to read. She sent him a glower. 'Are my eyes sad now?'

'Far from it. I think I should be worried.'

'Oh, I don't think very much worries you,' she drawled mockingly. 'There's little to choose between your skin and the hide of a rhinoceros.'

'On the contrary, you'd be surprised at what worries me, princess,' he countered smoothly.

'I'd certainly be surprised if you said anything made you lose sleep at night.'

'Then you'd be wrong,' Lance returned silkily, moving his leg so that it brushed hers. He heard her breath snag at the contact and smiled faintly. 'You could make me lose sleep, Kari Maitland, but I wouldn't begrudge it, for we would be doing something far more…exhilarating than sleeping.'

'Don't you ever stop?' she gasped, and his glance turned sultry.

'I'm not usually asked to. On the contrary,' he flirted.

Heat suffused her at the outrageous remark, but at the same time deep inside her something turned liquid. He was doing it again, turning her on with words and allowing her imagination to do the rest. She hadn't really ever thought of herself as a very sensual woman. She had enjoyed making love with Russ, but it had been pleasant rather than spectacular. He had never made her have vivid mental pictures of them entwined on a bed, simply by uttering a provocative word or two.

She forced herself to block out the image. 'You

know what they say. Self-praise is no recommendation.'

'So why don't you find out for yourself?' he suggested slyly. 'I'd be happy to oblige.'

She couldn't help but laugh. 'I just bet you would! Thanks, but I'll decline the offer.' Glancing at her watch, she was surprised to see it was gone eleven. 'It's getting late. I think we should leave,' she declared coolly.

'You know, you won't always chicken out,' he told her gently, and her heart leapt, though she did her best not to show it. Lance signalled the waiter and asked for the bill.

She knew he was baiting her, and refused to rise. 'I have to be at work early to accept a delivery.'

Lance rose and walked round to hold her chair for her. 'One day you'll give as good as you get,' he told her, and the power would swing her way. At the moment he unsettled her, but the instant she realised her power over him he would be lost. Not that he minded. In fact, he looked forward to it.

Kari stood and collected her purse, sending him an exasperated look. 'You... Oh, never mind. Just take me home. Please,' she added, when she saw the prompt forming on his tongue, and he laughed, sending tiny shivers chasing over her flesh.

'Come along, then. Never let it be said I disappointed a lady.'

Kari closed her eyes briefly at the connotation. The man was incorrigible!

It took them less than an hour to reach her home, and as soon as Lance stopped the car outside she turned to him with a cool smile. She was determined to make it clear that the evening ended here. She was not inviting him in for coffee—or anything else.

'Thank you again for what you did for Sarah,' she said, but instead of responding Lance released his seat belt and opened his door. 'What are you doing?' she asked uneasily, although she feared she knew. She had hoped to prevent this very thing.

Lance didn't answer until he had her door open. 'My mother always told me to see a lady to her door,' he said primly, and Kari was irritated to find herself torn between reluctant amusement and a childish wish to throw a temper tantrum.

'Your mother must have been a remarkable woman to put up with you,' she remarked dryly as she climbed out.

'She was,' Lance agreed, taking her elbow and steering her along the path to her door. 'She did her best to instil some gentlemanly virtues into me. Unfortunately she died whilst I was in high school and never did get to see the result of all her hard work.'

Kari heard the underlying sadness in his words, and was moved to respond to it. 'She would have been proud of you,' she told him truthfully. He might be the most annoying man she had ever met, but she could not deny he had good manners.

Lance smiled down at her, and his heart twisted at her sincere expression. 'Thanks. I like to think so too.'

Kari shook her head, wondering if her concern for him meant she was truly losing her mind. She should be keeping him at arm's length, not feeling his pain. 'You're a strange man. One minute you're making outrageous remarks, the next you're the perfect gentleman. I don't know what to make of you,' she declared, responding to his outstretched palm by producing her door keys and handing them over.

He hid a grin, knowing she hadn't really realised what she was doing. He doubted she had intended him to get so far. 'I'm not so hard to understand, Kari. Just like every other man, I put my pants on one leg at a time.'

She realised then how smoothly he had taken control, and sent him a narrow look. 'If you are like other men, how come you aren't on your way home already?'

He laughed. 'Just lucky, I guess.'

She shook her head. 'More like pigheaded. I don't think I should trust you.'

He used her keys to open her front door, then reached inside to switch on the light. They were instantly bathed in a warm golden glow. 'I intend to prove to you that I'm one man you can trust implicitly.' He took her hand and dropped her keys onto her palm, folding her fingers over them protectively.

'Why bother?' she countered coolly.

'Because I don't intend to just walk away from you, princess,' Lance declared candidly. 'I want you too much for that.'

'What about what I want? Doesn't that count?' she charged gruffly, and he shook his head wryly.

'Honey, you want the same thing, only you're still too teed off with me to admit it. So it looks as if I'm just going to have to prove it to you—again,' Lance pronounced long-sufferingly, taking her by the shoulders and urging her towards him.

Kari's eyes widened as she realised his intent. Her hand rose to his chest to ward him off. 'Wait. What do you think you're doing?' she gasped. This was most definitely not supposed to be happening.

'I'll give you three guesses,' he mocked, easily overcoming the restraint of her hand.

'But I don't want you to kiss me!' she protested faintly, eyes dropping to his mouth and lingering there as her throat closed over.

'Liar,' he taunted softly. 'Besides, you're forgetting something. You wanted to make amends for all the nasty, horrible things you said to me,' he reminded her.

'I didn't mean this!'

'Maybe not, but I told you you would have to do penance. The only thing I'll accept from you, Kari, is a kiss,' he informed her silkily, moving in to trap her between himself and the wall.

Her heart gave a wild lurch before galloping off madly. 'No. Absolutely not. You'll have to think of something else,' she refused breathlessly.

'Reneging, princess? This was your idea, remember. I was willing to drop the whole subject. You insisted. One kiss, Kari. Is that too much to ask?' he taunted gently.

She knew he wouldn't go until he had it, and she knew she only had herself to blame. 'Damn you,' she cursed him as he lowered his head to hers. He paused for a second with his lips a bare breath away from hers, as if giving her the option, then took her mouth.

His touch wreaked havoc with her senses the instant their lips touched. This was no gentle kiss. It scorched her, demanding a response she could not withhold. Her fingers tightened on the fabric of his jacket as his tongue stroked tantalisingly over her lips, until her rioting senses told her it was not enough. She wanted more, and with a faint, gasping moan she parted them and allowed him in. Not just allowed—welcomed. His tongue found sensitive areas that made her shudder with pleasure, and sent her thoughts packing. She could only feel, and when he sought her tongue she was helpless to do anything but meet him, stroke for silken stroke.

Tremors ran through her, and her knees suddenly buckled. She would have fallen, except Lance's arms were there, holding her, pulling her in to the hard contours of his body. She felt the evidence of his arousal and a moan escaped her. Oh, God, she wanted this man. Wanted him so much.

It showed in her eyes when Lance ended the kiss and eased away to look down at her. 'This isn't the end, it's only the beginning,' he told her huskily. 'Isn't it?'

Kari swallowed hard, staring up at him. 'I'm not inviting you in,' she said thickly.

He smiled at that, caressing her with his eyes. 'I know, but you will one day. I'm a patient man. I can wait. I'll go as slowly as you want me to.'

There was no sexual innuendo in his words. She knew he was telling her that she had control of their affair. How far they went and how fast was up to her. As if to emphasise the point, he released her and stepped back.

'Good night, princess. Sleep well.'

She couldn't find a voice to answer him with, and didn't know what she would have said anyway. She stared at him for one second longer, then turned on trembling limbs and went inside, closing the door behind her. Unable to go further, she leant back against the solid wood, breathing raggedly.

She knew she had got away lightly tonight. The thought of stopping had never entered her head. Every time they kissed, the effect was more powerful than the last. It was incredible how violently she responded to him. He sent her senses blazing out of control and she was beginning to crave it. He called to her in ways she hadn't imagined possible. It was stunning. He brought her alive, and she wanted to revel in it for as long as it lasted. Closing her eyes, she finally admitted to herself that she wasn't going to fight him any more.

On the other side of the door, Lance took several deep breaths in order to regain his control. It had been hard to step away from her, but he had known it was the right thing to do. In order to win her, he had to give her the freedom she needed to choose for herself. She was halfway to being in love with him already, and he didn't want to scare her off by being greedy. She would come to him—soon. All he had to do was be patient.

CHAPTER SIX

THE phone rang, and Kari jumped a good foot off the ground. She had been daydreaming again. She had had another restless night, her sleep laced with erotic dreams which had kept her tossing and turning. She would have felt a darn sight more rested if she had actually spent the night with Lance, rather than just dreaming about it, she thought wryly. It was no wonder her thoughts kept drifting, and she had trouble concentrating on her monthly accounts.

'Where were you last night?' Sarah asked without preamble the instant Kari answered.

'Out,' she responded noncommittally, and could almost hear her friend's mind whirring.

'Well, I know that. I tried calling and all I kept getting was the answer machine. Did he take you somewhere nice?' Sarah fished hopefully, but Kari wasn't biting.

'Why didn't you leave a message?'

'Why won't you tell me where you were?'

Kari knew from past experience she wasn't going to win this particular battle unless she hung up, and she couldn't do that. 'OK, if I tell you where I was, will you promise not to ask questions?'

'Sure,' Sarah said quickly, crossing her fingers.

'I was having dinner with Lance Kersee,' she confessed, and heard Sarah gasp.

'Kersee, as in the hotel people?'

'You've heard of them?' Kari asked in surprise.

'So would you have if you took your nose out of a book now and then,' her friend rejoined without malice. 'So tell me, how on earth did you meet him? Is he good looking?'

'I thought you weren't going to ask questions,' Kari challenged helplessly.

'I lied,' Sarah confessed blithely. 'Come on, give.'

With some reluctance, Kari explained all about the mix-up, and how Lance had insisted on taking her to dinner. There was a great deal she didn't reveal. Her response to the man wasn't something she wanted to share with anyone. It was private. Special.

'Hmm, sounds to me like you've hooked a live one. Don't you even dare consider throwing him back. Land him and take him home,' Sarah advised, clearly amused by the mess her friend had got herself into.

Kari rolled her eyes. She wondered what Sarah would say if she said she was considering it. She wouldn't dare, though. Sarah might be rendered momentarily speechless, but after that she would have plenty to say, and Kari wasn't prepared to answer those sort of searching questions.

Right then Jenny bounced in with a huge grin on her face. 'Parcel for you, Kari,' she said brightly, and deposited a long oblong box on the desk in front of her employer.

Seeing it, Kari felt her heart do an intricate little dance. She knew a florist's box when she saw one. 'Oh,' she gasped faintly.

'What is it? What's going on?' Sarah barked down the line.

'Hold on,' Kari told her, setting the phone down and staring at the gold box as if it might leap up and bite her at any moment.

She hesitated a fraction of a second before reaching out and removing the lid, folding back layers of tissue paper. Her lips parted on a tiny gasp as her incredulous gaze fell on a dozen perfectly matched long-stem pink roses. There was no card, but she didn't need one to know who they were from. They were beautiful, and the scent as she bent over the box was heady. They must have cost a small fortune.

'Oh, wow!' Jenny exclaimed in awe. 'This guy is serious,' she added, then, as it was clear her boss wasn't listening, she turned and went back into the shop with an envious sigh.

Kari meanwhile scrabbled for the phone. 'He sent me roses,' she told her friend in consternation.

'Really? What colour?'

'Pink.'

'Sounds like he's trying to tell you something,' Sarah observed gleefully. 'Are you sure *you're* telling *me* everything, Kari Maitland?' she queried mischievously, and Kari dragged her hand through her hair in exasperation.

'I'm telling you everything I intend to tell you!' she returned sweetly, and put the phone down before her friend could utter another word.

Leaning her arms on the desk, she rested her chin on her hands and frowned at the inoffensive box. Why was he was sending her flowers? This thing between her and Lance was purely sex. It didn't need romantic gestures. Yet, knowing him, it was clearly the kind of thing he would do. He was a gentleman, and gentlemen gave flowers to their lovers. Which was what she would be any day now.

The phone rang again, and she answered it automatically.

'Did you like the roses?'

Her back straightened reflexively as she recognised the voice, whilst the silky sound of it made her toes curl. She had never met anyone who could sound so sexy saying the most mundane thing the way Lance did.

Because of it, she found she had to clear her throat in order to speak. 'They're beautiful.'

'Good,' he said, and she could hear him smile. 'I saw them and they reminded me of you.'

'Prickly, you mean?' Kari retorted sardonically, and Lance laughed. She closed her eyes as shivers ran over her skin. Even over the phone he was devastating.

'You may be prickly, Kari, but I know you'll respond to careful handling. You'll have all the care and attention I can lavish on you,' he returned seductively.

She caught her breath as her heart lurched slightly. 'You're very good at this, aren't you?'

'Sending flowers?' he teased.

'Seduction.'

'Ah.' There was a cautious edge to that simple word and Kari smiled wryly as she picked up one of the waxy blooms and brushed it over her cheek.

'I'm thinking you must have had lots of practice,' she mused.

'Some, but there's no need to be jealous, sweetheart. You have my undivided attention now.'

Kari found that now she had accepted the inevitable there was an added spice to their verbal sparring that she was beginning to like very much. 'You talk a good game. I hope you live up to expectations.' She could tell her flirting had surprised him by the sudden silence at the end of the line. He rallied quickly, however.

'I promise you won't be disappointed, princess,' he vowed huskily, and to Kari the nickname no longer sounded derogatory, but was more like a caress.

She found she liked the sound of it.

'I'm glad you stopped fighting it, princess,' he told her next, his voice no longer teasing but sounding surprisingly serious.

'Me too,' she admitted softly, and heard his sharp intake of breath.

'Damn, you would say that when it's impossible for me to do what I want to do!' he growled and she laughed huskily.

'What do you want to do?'

At the other end of the line, Lance shivered at the scintillating question. 'Kiss you for starters.'

'Mmm, sounds good.'

Lance started laughing. 'Hell, I had no idea you were such a terrible tease. You're doing it on purpose, aren't you?'

Kari grinned to herself. She was finding that she

had unsuspected depths when it came to flirting with Lance Kersee. 'I have absolutely no idea what you're talking about. Now, I have to go. There are customers waiting.' It was a lie, but he didn't know that.

'Wait!' he called out hurriedly. 'I rang to say, much as I want to see you tonight, I have a dinner engagement I can't get out of.'

She was surprised to feel a rush of disappointment, which was silly. She had no claims on him. 'I understand.'

'I'll call you tomorrow,' he promised.

'I'll look forward to it.'

Lance rang off and she replaced the receiver slowly. Well, she had burned her boats now. There was no going back. She found the idea didn't scare her half as much as she had thought it would. She was going to enjoy the affair for as long as it lasted and when it was over she would simply get on with her life once more.

When Sunday came, Kari found herself carrying out her usual routine of cleaning up and doing the laundry. When she discovered she had dusted the same room twice simply because the telephone was there, she was disgusted with herself. She absolutely was not going to hang around indoors waiting for the phone to ring like a teenager with a crush. It was a beautifully sunny day outside, perfect for doing the garden chores she had been putting off. Besides, if she left the back door propped open she was bound to hear the phone if it did ring. So she changed into

shorts and an old T-shirt and sallied forth barefoot
to weed the flower beds and dead-head the roses.

Lance found her there an hour later, when he
walked round the side of the house after his knock
had gone unanswered. The sight of her long bare legs
brought a lazy grin to his lips, and he propped himself against the corner of the building to watch her.
She stretched, and her legs tensed to take the strain,
sending his pulse rocketing. She was driving him
crazy. If he didn't have her in his bed soon, he might
just go out of his mind.

He must have made some noise, for she looked
round suddenly, nearly overbalanced, and grasped
the rosebush to steady herself. He winced as he heard
her yelp, and pushed himself upright, walking towards her.

Kari sucked her stinging thumb and watched him
cover the ground in long, lazy strides. Her heart
knocked and her mouth went dry when she saw what
he was wearing. Those jeans were positively sinful.
They moulded every muscle and sinew and made her
go hot all over. A slow, throbbing ache started up
way down inside her, and her stomach clenched on
a powerful wave of desire. Dear God, but she wanted
this man. Just seeing him brought her senses to tingling life. He hadn't touched her, and yet she could
feel her nipples hardening to painfully sensitive nubs
in response to the sheer animal magnetism of him. It
wasn't any wonder her breathing went haywire as he
came to a halt before her.

Easily reading her expression, Lance wanted to
haul her into his arms and kiss her breathless, but he

didn't. He did his best to calm the raging heat her eyes had engendered in him. He had nearly gone up in flames, the way she had looked at him. As if she had wanted to eat him up.

'Did you hurt yourself?' he asked gruffly. 'You should be more careful,' he added, reaching for her hand to examine the tiny puncture mark.

His head lowered and Kari found herself staring at tantalising waves of lush dark hair. She battled the urge to run her fingers through it. 'I was doing OK until you arrived. You startled me,' she admitted, then held her breath as she watched him raise her hand to his lips. 'What are you doing?' she queried in a strangled voice as his lips caressed the spot. He glanced up at her.

'Kissing it better,' he returned thickly, watching her eyes change from calm blue to turbulent ultramarine. He straightened but didn't release her. 'How does it feel now?' Without waiting for an answer, Lance drew her thumb into his mouth and stroked it with his tongue.

Kari stifled a moan as her system went into overload. She turned molten inside. It felt as if he had touched every inch of her skin. She hadn't known that such a simple act could be so erotic. She shivered, and struggled to maintain some sense of reality. They were in the middle of her garden, for heaven's sake. In full view of anyone who happened to be watching. With a strangled gasp she pulled her hand away, crossing her arms to stop herself from reaching out to him as she wanted to do.

'I thought you were going to phone,' she said breathlessly.

'I was, but then I realised I wanted to see you, not hear the sound of your voice,' he admitted honestly, watching the fabric of her T-shirt pull tight across her breasts, revealing the aroused nubs that he longed to feel against his palms. 'Are you pleased to see me?'

Kari followed the direction of his gaze. When she saw what he was seeing, she thought it must be patently obvious how she felt. She had missed him, and they were too far apart. To hell with the neighbours. Let them think what they liked. She stepped towards him with a long, steady look. 'What do you think?'

Lance smiled slowly and gave in to the temptation which had been riding him, hauling her into his arms where she belonged. His breath left him in a rush at the contact. God, but she felt good. She was pressed against him from shoulder to toe, and the pleasure made him feel a little light-headed. She had that effect on him. He knew she always would. He folded his arms about her and closed his eyes.

Yes, Kari thought as she came into contact with the hard male length of him. Her body softened, moulding itself to him. A soft moan of pleasure escaped her lips, and her eyelids fluttered down. He felt every bit as good as she had known he would. Without volition, her hands found his shoulders and traced their broadness with trembling fingers. He was so big and strong, and yet he held her so very gently.

She felt his fingers in her hair, felt their gentle pressure tipping her head back, and found herself looking into a pair of intense grey eyes that seemed to bore into her very soul. Yet only for a second, for in the next instant his mouth was on hers, and the world spun away. Her lips parted, allowing him access to her mouth, and she shuddered at the insistent thrust of his tongue. She met it with her own, joining in a sensual game that left her drugged and gasping when they reluctantly broke the searing contact in order to breathe.

Her head fell back as his lips found her neck, and she arched to his touch. She felt his hands fumbling with the bottom of her T-shirt, then he was touching her, his palms scorching her as they glided upwards. She held her breath, her fingers curling into the fabric of his shirt as she waited for him to find her breasts. She ached for his touch, and when he claimed the jutting peaks, teasing her nipples with his thumbs, a piercing tide of pleasure shafted down to the core of her.

Lance heard her whimper of pleasure and had to hold on to his sanity. God, but she did things to him no other woman had ever done. He had never felt such a powerful craving. He needed to make her his. Wanted to make them one in such a way that she would never feel whole unless she was with him. It was male and primitive, and it brought him within an ace of taking her down to the grass and making it happen.

It took all of his not inconsiderable strength to draw back from the edge, and it left him aching. 'I want you so much!' he declared thickly against her throat, his voice hot and heavy with passion.

'I want you too,' Kari confessed with a groan.

Lance stared down into her drugged eyes, breathing heavily. 'I think maybe we should stop before this gets out of hand,' he murmured unevenly.

'Or we could go inside,' she suggested huskily, now that her mind was made up not wanting to wait any longer.

His heart slammed in his chest at her words, and he went still. 'Are you sure?'

Her mouth curved into a sultry smile and she reached up to run a finger over his lips. 'Oh, yes,' she breathed, and gasped when he made a growling sound in his throat and reached down to sweep her up into his arms. She held on, burying her face in his neck as he strode with her towards the house. This was what she wanted. What she had wanted ever since she had laid eyes on him.

'Which way?' he asked as they reached the top of the stairs, and she pointed out her room on the right. He carried her inside and kicked the door closed with his foot. Only then did he lower her to her feet. 'There's still time to change your mind,' he told her, but Kari shook her head.

'I want to make love with you. Now,' she insisted, reaching for the hem of her T-shirt, tugging it off and tossing it aside. Then she turned to the buttons of his shirt and began to undo them with fumbling fingers.

Lance drew in a deep breath as heat rushed to his loins. Gritting his teeth against the power of his desire, he brushed her hands aside, dealing with the fastenings and tossing his shirt to join hers. In the next instant she was back in his arms, her hands running over his back, sending shivers down his spine, whilst her lips found one of his nipples and teased it with her tongue until he couldn't hold back a groan of pleasure. His body surged, and he caught hold of her hips, pulling her up into him so that she could feel the strength of his arousal.

Kari moaned softly, parting her legs a little to settle herself more fully against him, rocking back and forth in instinctive search for satisfaction. Then his hands were at the fastening of her shorts, undoing them, pushing them down together with her panties. She could feel his hands moulding her bottom as he ground himself against her, and it wasn't enough. She wanted more. She wanted to feel him inside her, filling her. Now. She didn't want finesse. She just wanted him and she didn't want to wait. Her hand fumbled for the button of his jeans, then pushed down the zipper.

Lance's breath hissed in through his teeth as he felt her fingers close around him, and he very nearly exploded right there. He gritted his teeth and struggled for control, reaching between them to catch her wrist.

'Wait!' he gasped out.

Her lips found his, kissing him into silence. 'I don't want to wait. I want you now.'

Her plea was enough to make him lose the battle for control. With a guttural cry he pushed her onto the bed, spared just enough time to shuck off his jeans, and followed her down. He entered her in one powerful thrust and Kari welcomed him with a cry of pleasure. She felt him tense, trying to retain a semblance of control, but she didn't want that. She wanted his fire, and she folded her legs around him, taking him deeper into her, rocking her hips in a rhythm he had to follow.

The passion was too intense to last long. Her climax took her swiftly, and as she spun off the edge of the world she felt his release as he joined her.

Lance collapsed on top of her, closing his eyes as he fought for breath. He felt stunned by the force of their passion. He had never come close to feeling anything like it before. She was incredible. He had suspected it, but he could never have imagined the reality. Raising his head, he shifted his weight so that it was no longer fully on her. He regretted that he hadn't given her the long, slow loving he'd intended for their first time together, but she hadn't given him much choice. A reminiscent smile hovered on his lips as he ran his hand along the curve of her hip.

Kari sighed at his touch and turned her head. 'What are you smiling at?' she asked, one hand lifting to smooth over his chest.

His eyes glowed hotly as he gazed into hers. 'Just wondering if you were always that insistent,' he observed wryly, then winced as her fingers caught in his chest hair and tugged gently.

'Only when I know what I want,' she confessed huskily. 'Are you sorry?'

He shook his head. 'Hell, no.'

Kari stretched like a cat and sighed contentedly. 'Good.'

Lance laughed aloud, turning and making himself

comfortable against the pillows, pulling her into the curve of his body. She fitted as if she had been made for him. Which he knew she had.

'This wasn't quite how I intended to spend the morning,' he told her, and felt her smile.

'No?' Kari queried, unable to recall when she had felt so relaxed and happy.

'I was going to take you on a picnic. There's food in the car.'

She twisted to look at him, her chin resting over his heart. 'We can always have it here,' she proposed. 'I'm sure we could find a way to…work up an appetite,' she added suggestively, and Lance felt himself grow hard again at the thought of how they would achieve that.

Quick as a flash he rolled over, pinning her beneath him. 'Are you a witch?' he asked with a growl, and Kari smiled when she felt the evidence of his response.

'I can tell you think it's a good idea,' she declared impishly, moving against him deliberately. She felt quite deliciously wanton.

Lance bent over her, taking her nipple into his mouth and biting it gently with his teeth until he heard her gasp of pleasure, then laved it with his tongue until it hardened to an aching point which had her shifting restlessly beneath him. Only then did he look into her eyes again. They were a deep, sensual blue.

'Do you know what I'm thinking right now, princess?' he teased against her lips.

Kari shivered in anticipation. She wanted him

again, and the amazing thing was the need was as strong as it had been before. 'That food can wait?' she guessed.

'Got it in one,' he growled and took her mouth.

They didn't eat until a long time later, then they cleared up and made love again, falling asleep in each other's arms. Kari woke first. It was getting dark, and she wondered what time it was. Lance was sprawled on his stomach, fast asleep. She lay looking at him, unable to regret what had passed between them. It had been too beautiful. *He* was beautiful. She could simply lie there looking at him endlessly, except that she realised just how thirsty she was. She would go downstairs and get them something cold to drink. Sliding off the bed, she picked up Lance's shirt and slipped it on, rolling up the sleeves to fit. Trying not to disturb him, she tiptoed out of the room and down the stairs.

Switching on the kitchen light, she realised the back door was still open. She bit her lip. They had been so lost in each other, anyone could have walked in and burgled the place. She would have to be more careful in future. Fetching herself a can of juice from the fridge, she padded out onto the back porch and curled up in a corner of the swing, using one foot to set herself moving slowly backwards and forwards.

She felt…different. More alive. Lance had done that. He was an incredible lover. Just thinking about him brought her out in gooseflesh. Strangely, she felt as if she had known him a long time, not just a matter of days. Being with him gave her a buzz as nothing else did. From the way they responded to each other, she doubted this was an affair which would burn out quickly. She was going to enjoy every single minute of it.

Hearing a sound, she glanced round. Lance stood in the doorway. He had slipped into his jeans but hadn't bothered to fasten them. Her breath snagged in her throat. God, but he was so damned sexy, he turned her knees to jelly.

'Did I wake you?' she asked him as he yawned and stretched and ambled over to join her.

'Nope,' he denied, placing an arm along the swing back behind her. 'You OK?' He had missed her warmth in his sleep. That was what had roused him. When he had discovered her sitting out here, his first thought had been that she had regrets. He wasn't sure how he would handle it if she did. To him their loving couldn't have been more perfect.

'I'm fine,' she told him in a scratchy voice, because the heat from his body was already doing those wonderful things to her again.

Lance decided he had to broach the subject for his own peace of mind. 'Regretting it, princess?' he asked gently, stroking one finger lazily down the nape of her neck.

She looked at him out of the corner of her eyes, a feline smile curving her lips. 'Uh-uh.'

Relief brought a smile, and he made himself more comfortable beside her. The night sounds settled round them as they sat in comfortable silence. Lance could think of nothing better than sitting with her like this every night for the next fifty or sixty years.

'Did you live here with your husband?' he asked

curiously, and heard her sigh heavily. 'Do you mind talking about him?'

'No,' she said, and it was true. She didn't mind talking about Russ to him. 'We lived in Ohio where Russ had his practice. I bought this house when I moved back here after he died.'

Lance couldn't help being relieved. He hadn't much liked the idea of sharing a house with a ghost. 'He was a doctor?'

Kari smiled and shook her head. 'Not exactly. Russ was a vet. He loved animals. We both did.' She had had her horses, and the cross-country races that she had loved so much. Somewhere in the cellar there was a box with all the rosettes she had won in it.

'How did you meet him?'

'I'd known him all my life. We virtually grew up together. I lived with my grandparents next door.' Russ had been older than her, and he had treated her like a kid sister. As she'd grown older, affection had turned to something warmer, and all her dreams had come true when he had asked her to marry him. She hadn't hesitated.

'What happened to your own parents?'

'They died in a car wreck. Somebody overran a stop sign. I was six and inconsolable when I came to live with Grandma and Grandpa. Russ took me under his wing. I think I fell in love with him right then.'

'He was your childhood sweetheart?' Lance queried gently. He could not mind the fact of Russ, for he was her past. Kari loved him now. She couldn't have made love to him the way she had and not love him. She just didn't realise it yet.

'I guess you could say that,' she agreed. 'What about you? Did you have a childhood sweetheart?' she teased, and he grinned roguishly.

'Bobbie Sue Palmer. She blacked my eye once,' he remarked reminiscently and Kari laughed.

'I hate to ask what you were doing to make her hit you,' she drawled mockingly.

Lance shot her a hurt look. 'Nothing. I swear my intentions up in that hayloft were totally innocent,' he declared and Kari snorted.

'I don't think your intentions have been innocent since you took your first breath!'

'You've been talking to my sister, haven't you?' he accused lightly.

Kari couldn't help but laugh again. 'I don't need to talk to her, I can see what you are for myself. Mind you, I wouldn't mind comparing notes some time,' she added thoughtfully.

'That's great. You've never met her, but already you're on her side. I don't stand a chance, do I?'

'Nope,' she agreed, grinning up at him, and he did the only thing he could. He kissed her. It was swift but thorough, and it left her breathless and aching for more. 'What was that for?' she asked when he released her.

'Just acting on impulse.'

Kari's eyes gleamed in the darkness, and she set her drink aside, twisting onto her knees and quickly straddling him. Smiling, she ran her hands over his broad chest, delighting in the feel of him. She found his flat male nipples and teased them with her nails, loving the way he moaned way down deep in his throat.

'Have you got an impulse to do something now?' she queried throatily, dipping her head to lap up the droplet of moisture which had formed at the base of his throat.

Lance put his arms around her and stood in one swift motion. 'Oh, yes, princess, I surely do,' he declared hotly, and carried her back inside.

It was ages before either of them remembered that they still hadn't locked the back door.

CHAPTER SEVEN

KARI hummed to herself as she sorted through the boxes of books she had bought at a house sale just that morning. There were a good few first editions which would sell well, and even if they didn't she doubted it would spoil her mood. She had been in a euphoric state of mind for the past four weeks.

The exact four weeks that she and Lance had been lovers. It was fascinating what truly incredible sex could do for the disposition. They were still hungry for each other, and the bubble didn't look like bursting any time soon. Which was fine by her.

Not that they fell into bed the instant they saw each other. Not always, anyway, she admitted with a grin. Lance had taken her out to dinner several times, and they had gone to the theatre more than once. They had taken to spending every free moment together, and it was during those times that they discovered how similar their tastes were. They liked the same food, the same music, and even the same weather. Both enjoyed driving out to some quiet spot along the coast on a blustery day and walking for miles with the wind and the salt spray in their hair.

A faintly wicked smile curved her lips. Of course, *then* they would come home and rip each other's clothes off, she admitted, laughing to herself at the memory.

'Somebody's happy,' Jenny remarked with a grin as she popped into the office for a new roll of tape to put in the dispenser on the counter.

Kari glanced up, grinning back. 'You could be right,' she agreed cheerily. Dissembling was useless when she had been grinning like a Cheshire cat for days now.

Jenny sighed dramatically. 'Don't you just love being in love?'

Kari's whole system seemed to give an almighty jolt at the teasing words, and her grin vanished. Her head shot up again. 'What did you say?' she charged faintly, and her assistant gave her an old-fashioned look.

'I said, don't you love being in love?' Jenny repeated obligingly, then, when the other woman didn't respond, clucked her tongue. 'Come on, Kari, everyone knows you're in love with the man. It sticks out a mile.'

Kari felt herself pale and her heart started to beat unevenly. 'Don't be silly! Of course I'm not in love with Lance. I'm not in love with anybody,' she denied the idea with a wobbly laugh. 'Whatever gave you that idea?'

'You did. You act as if you're in love,' Jenny explained dryly, and Kari frowned.

'That's ridiculous. I'm not behaving any differently,' she denied hastily, and, after giving her employer a strange look, Jenny shrugged.

'If you say so, boss,' she muttered with a roll of the eyes, and departed again with the roll of tape.

Kari stared after her with a sinking feeling in her

stomach. It was ridiculous. Of course she wasn't acting as if she were in love! She wouldn't! Loving
someone—anyone—wasn't on her agenda. She
glanced down at her hands and found they were
shaking. She curled them into fists to stop the fine
tremors. Of all the stupid things for Jenny to say!
Love? They were all crazy. She was just feeling
good. They had simply misinterpreted her reaction to
a healthy dose of good sex.

Hadn't they?

She pressed a hand to a suddenly roiling stomach.
They must have. She could not have fallen in love
with Lance. It just wasn't possible. She admitted to
liking him a lot. She enjoyed being with him, and
their sex life was pretty spectacular, but that didn't
mean anything. It certainly didn't mean love. You
didn't have to love someone to enjoy being with
them. This bubbly feeling she had been experiencing
lately was just because she felt good. *It was not love.*

Kari found she was clenching her teeth so hard it
was making her head ache. It took a conscious effort
on her part to make herself relax. She took several
deep, calming breaths and walked into the small
kitchen area to switch on the kettle, going through
the motions of making herself a cup of herb tea.
When it was ready she took it back to her desk and
sat down, cradling the hot cup in her chilly hands.

She felt restless and uneasy, when only moments
ago she had been feeling so good. Damn it, she
shouldn't have let a few silly words destroy her
mood so utterly. Only she knew how she felt. She
was making too much of it. Unfortunately now the

words had been spoken she could not stop them playing over and over in her head, and the horrifying thought that there might be a grain of truth in them was what set her nerves jangling. Yet it couldn't be true. OK, so she hadn't been able to get him out of her mind from the moment they'd met, but that didn't mean she loved him.

If for even one second she began to suspect she might be in danger of stepping over the boundary she had set herself she would have to stop seeing him. There would be no other alternative. The thought sent her heart plunging to her boots, for she knew she wasn't ready to end it yet. Nor did she have to, she insisted staunchly, because Jenny and the rest of them had it wrong. The relationship she had with Lance was purely sexual. She wanted him and he wanted her. The feeling was mutual, and it was lust, not love. Love had never ever been mentioned.

Her heart slowly settled back to its normal rhythm. It wasn't love. It was good old-fashioned lust. She could continue seeing Lance without fear. He was nothing more than a man she liked a lot, and who just happened to be a truly fantastic lover. She wasn't going to let this trouble her any longer. She knew what she felt and what she didn't, and that was all that mattered.

'I do not love Lance Kersee,' she said out loud, and instantly felt better for it. She was making a mountain out of a molehill. The best thing she could do now was forget all about it.

In fact, she had put it from her mind completely

by the time they drove up the coast for dinner at a restaurant famous for its seafood a few evenings later. The heat had been oppressive all day, almost thundery, and Kari was looking forward to the clean fresh air. Yet from the outset she knew something was wrong. Lance was unusually distracted during the drive, sometimes seeming miles away. Throughout dinner he made a determined effort to be cheerful, but it didn't ring true, and he barely touched his food. Her stomach began to tie itself in knots.

Whatever was wrong, it was serious. 'Not hungry?' she probed carefully, unable to shake the feeling that something bad was going to happen.

Lance pushed his plate away and shook his head. 'It's too hot to eat.'

Actually, he had lost his appetite round about five o'clock that afternoon when he had made his last call to Denver. He had spent the better part of the day on the telephone trying to put off a decision he should have made a week ago. He had finished the business he had taken on here and should have left for Denver already, but he had been delaying his departure. Ordinarily his deputy could handle matters once a plan of operation had been agreed, but the owner of the firm who had called him in was digging in his heels over implementing vital changes and Lance was the only one capable of making him see reason. He had to go, but it meant leaving Kari, and that was not a prospect he looked forward to with pleasure.

Leaning his elbows on the table, Lance rested his chin on his hands and watched her broodingly over them. 'You're a very beautiful woman, you know,' he declared in a kind of husky growl, and her heart kicked.

She batted her lashes demurely. 'You say the most wonderful things.'

His teeth flashed whitely as he laughed. 'I aim to please.'

'Oh, you do. You do,' Kari responded coquettishly, and he chuckled.

'God, I'm going to miss you!' he exclaimed gruffly, and Kari felt her smile freeze on her face.

'Miss me?' she queried faintly, and her heart sank when she watched his face settle into grim lines.

Taking out his wallet, Lance tossed some notes onto the table and stood up. 'Let's take a walk along the beach, princess. There's something I have to say to you,' he told her tersely.

Kari swallowed hard and rose to join him, her thoughts rioting. What did he mean he was going to miss her? It seemed to suggest that he was going somewhere—without her. The further they got from the lights of the restaurant, the more certain she grew. He was leaving, and this was the end of their affair.

The possibility caused her dinner to lie uneasily on her stomach as she realised she wasn't ready for it to end. Of course, she had always known it would have to end some time. His job took him all over the world, and it was foolish to imagine he would linger here when his job was done. It was the suddenness of it which had shocked her. That was why she felt so upset. She had thought they would have longer together. However, she was a sensible, mature woman. If it had to be, then she would accept it with a good grace. Only she would rather not be kept waiting for the axe to fall.

'Why don't you tell me what's on your mind, Lance?' she suggested in a slightly wobbly voice.

He had been dreading this moment, but he knew he wasn't doing either of them any favours by putting it off. 'I have to leave,' he told her shortly, and felt her sigh.

Her heart slammed into her chest, and she licked lips which had gone dry. So, this was it. 'When?' she asked coolly, determined to behave with dignity.

Lance frowned a little at her response. He had expected her to be just a little upset. 'Day after tomorrow.'

Her stomach fell away this time. So soon? 'I see,' she said faintly.

He stopped walking and turned to her, his hands resting on her shoulders. 'I'd take you with me, but...'

Kari didn't feel much like smiling but she forced one to her lips. She would not make this difficult for him. 'That's OK, I couldn't leave the shop anyway.'

'I don't know how soon I can get back here,' Lance went on, his thumbs starting an unconscious caress. God, she was beautiful. The thought of leaving her for even a short while cut like a knife in his heart.

She gave a tiny offhand shrug. 'You don't have to explain anything to me. I always knew you would have to go eventually,' she said evenly. They were both adults. She had walked into this with her eyes wide open, expecting nothing more than she had got. He didn't have to beat himself up about it.

He smiled crookedly. 'Are you always this understanding?'

'I try to be,' she confessed softly, closing the distance and slipping her arms around him. If they only had two days, she didn't want to waste a minute of it. Standing on tiptoe, she pressed her lips to his, coaxing his to part with her tongue. The sound he made in his throat brought a smile to her lips. His kiss was deep and thorough, leaving her wanting more. She loved the way he held nothing back. He was generous and passionate, and she would miss him when he went.

'Let's go home,' she sighed. 'I want to make love to you.'

Lance's mind was running on the same track. He still had things to say, but later would do. Much later, when his brain was functioning clearly again. Right now, all he could think of was making love to her until they were both sated.

There was an extra quality to their lovemaking that night, a kind of quiet intensity. It lifted them higher than they had ever gone before, and their climax was so powerful it left them both breathless and barely able to move. It was Lance who recovered first. Shifting onto his back, he reached out a lazy arm and drew her into his side. Kari sighed, her body still pulsing, hooking one leg over his thigh. She smiled faintly when she heard him laugh softly.

'Honey, after that, you're just going to have to marry me,' he declared huskily.

Though her heart skipped at the declaration, she knew he didn't mean it. He was leaving, after all. 'You don't have to go that far,' she countered teasingly.

Lance's hand slowly caressed the curve of her hip. He wasn't surprised she didn't take him seriously, for the question of marriage had never come up. In fact, they'd never talked about the future at all. However, it was what he wanted, and he knew she would want it too. After all, they loved each other. Marriage was the next step in their relationship.

He had intended asking her earlier but they had got sidetracked. He grinned at the memory of the route they had taken. But they were back on track now and he didn't want to wait any longer. If he had to leave Kari for a while, he wanted his ring safely on her finger before he went, to confirm his commitment. He didn't want her in any doubt that their relationship was permanent.

'Hey, I'm serious, princess. I want you to marry me. I love you,' he told her in a voice made husky by emotion. He was totally unprepared for the sudden tension which ripped through her.

Kari felt chilled from her head to her toes. She jerked away from him, sitting up to stare at him through horrified blue eyes. 'What did you say?' she asked hoarsely.

Startled by her reaction, Lance sat up too. 'I said I love you, and want to marry you,' he repeated, very much aware that something had just gone badly wrong with his plan. He had assumed, obviously naively, that she would be delighted to hear him confess his love for her, but her reaction was saying quite the opposite.

A trembling started up inside her, and she reached out to tug the corner of the sheet around her almost angrily. Why was he talking about love? This had never been about love! 'You can't love me!' she gasped, appalled at the idea. 'This is absurd. I know we feel the same way about each other, so you can't possibly love me!' For if he did, that would mean... She shied away from the thought.

Lance's heart took a crazy lurch. He was losing the plot. 'I can. I do. It was love at first sight for me. I thought it was the same for you,' he ground out tersely, and Kari stared at him, aghast.

'How could you think that?' she gasped hoarsely.

Lance stared at her blankly. How? Could she really not know how she was when she was with him? Clearly she could, and it was up to him to make her see what was right there in front of her. 'Why shouldn't I think that? Your eyes tell me you love me all the time, and when we make love your body says the same thing. I may be wrong about a lot of things, but I know you couldn't make love to me the way you do without loving me,' he told her simply.

Her throat closed over. 'Th-that's not true!' she protested faintly. But as she looked at him it was as if a veil were suddenly lifted from her eyes. All at once she saw herself as others did, and the result was irrefutable and devastating.

'Oh, God,' she whispered, closing her eyes as she was hit by the uncompromising truth. He was right. She could not have made love to him as she had unless she loved him. History told her that. She had only made love with one other man, and she had loved him, too. In order to give herself, she had to love. It was that simple and that terrible.

She had done the one thing she had sworn never to do. If he had said nothing she might have gone on in blissful ignorance. Would have kept kidding herself that she hadn't fallen in love with him. Not now. His words had stripped the blinkers from her eyes.

She shivered, feeling cold to her soul. How could she have been so foolish as to allow it to happen? She pressed her lips together tightly, knowing the question was redundant. The how wasn't important. It had happened, and now it had to end. She couldn't allow it to go on. Couldn't allow herself to care for him the way he was telling her he cared for her. Fear shafted through her. She dared not risk loving him. She couldn't do it. Couldn't take the chance.

'Kari?' Lance reached out to touch her shoulder gently, but she jumped as if scalded and flinched away.

'Why did you have to say that?' she cried through a painfully tight throat. Why couldn't he have left well enough alone? Now she was going to have to hurt him. There was no other way, because he loved her. She had to end it because she wouldn't love him, and there was no way of doing so without inflicting pain. If only she hadn't been so blind! But it was too late for that.

Lance had watched the play of emotions across her face with a sinking heart. Now he shook his head dazedly. 'What do you mean, why?' he challenged, keeping a tight rein on his own escalating emotions. 'Good God, woman, I love you! I know you love me, too.' How had he ended up in this nightmare?

Kari's fingers curled so tightly into the sheet, she was in danger of tearing it. 'Stop saying that! This isn't the way it's supposed to be!' she exclaimed tautly.

His eyes narrowed at that. What on earth was going on here? 'I wasn't supposed to love you or want to marry you?'

She swallowed painfully. 'No.'

Lance took in a careful breath before asking the other important question. 'And you weren't supposed to love me?' he charged, and she looked at him then, her eyes wild with emotion.

'I never said I loved you. Not once!' she denied harshly. Nor was she ever going to say it. She couldn't. Not ever again.

About to take issue with that, Lance caught himself up when he realised exactly what she had said. She hadn't said she didn't love him, just that she had never said she did. The difference was subtle but significant. Nothing here was as it seemed, and it would be in his own best interests to proceed with caution. He didn't know what can of worms he had opened up, but something told him his future happiness depended on him finding out.

'Tell me something, princess, what exactly did you think these past few weeks were all about?' he charged angrily, acting the way he knew she expected him to.

She shivered, hating to cause him pain. 'Sex,' she managed to choke out.

'Sex? You thought all there was between us was sex?' If he didn't sense she was lying that would have knocked the wind out of him.

Too caught up in her own misery to realise he didn't look as angry as he sounded, Kari nodded stiffly. 'What else?'

His eyes narrowed as another potential killer blow rebounded off him. 'It never occurred to you that I might have fallen in love with you?'

'No.' Dear Lord, she had been so blind! So wilfully, recklessly blind!

He stared at her for a second or two in silence, then climbed off the bed, pulled on his jeans in two angry movements and stalked to the window. Standing there looking out at the darkness, he dragged both hands through his hair. If he was wrong, if he was misreading the whole situation, he was storing up a whole parcel of grief for himself, yet he didn't think he was. All he had to go on was his gut instinct. For reasons he couldn't even begin to fathom she wasn't going to admit loving him. In fact, if he wasn't mistaken, she was about to cut him out of her life entirely. That he was not about to let happen, but first he had to prove his theory.

Squaring his shoulders, he turned to look at her. 'Enough of this, princess. You love me. I know you do,' he declared forcefully, picking his route carefully.

Her heart knocked painfully. 'I never told you that!' she protested again, wanting him to stop this.

Though she didn't know it, her oblique denials were giving him the signal to go on. 'You didn't have to tell me. I know it—here.' His fist thudded his chest over his heart, and she winced at his certainty.

'No. You're wrong. I would never let myself love you!' she denied quickly, eyes rounding as she heard what she had said and saw him pick up on it instantly.

His heart started beating in double-quick time. That unwary statement was all he needed to hear to convince him he was on the right track. He strode to the bed, catching her by the shoulders and dragging her to her feet. 'Wouldn't let yourself? What does that mean?'

She swallowed a large ball of emotion which threatened to choke her. 'It means I won't love you and I won't marry you!'

Unconsciously Lance's fingers bit into her flesh. There it was again. Won't love him. *Won't?* 'Why not, Kari? Why won't you love me?' he asked gruffly.

Kari gritted her teeth, knowing she was making a hash of it, but unable to back down. She had to protect herself. 'What difference does it make why?'

'A hell of a lot if you expect me to walk away from you. Don't you get it, princess? Won't implies you do love me, not that you don't,' he argued with instinctive care, and felt the shudder which went through her at his words. His heart contracted. She was shaking fit to bust, and all because he kept insisting she loved him. Looking into her eyes, he saw.

stark terror there. It nearly killed him. 'Honey, what are you so afraid of?'

Her lashes dropped, shielding her thoughts from his all-too-knowing eyes. Right now she was terribly afraid that he would somehow persuade her away from the course she knew she must take. He could do it, and then where would she be? Living in dread and fear of the moment when her world would shatter again. She couldn't do it.

The knowledge gave her the strength to tear herself free of his hold, and she staggered back on trembling legs. Grabbing up her robe from the chair, she fumbled it on, tying the belt tight. Only then, feeling marginally less vulnerable, did she face him again.

'I'm sorry if I hurt you, but it wasn't intentional. I never would have got involved with you if I knew you felt the way you did,' she said in a carefully controlled voice.

Lance could almost see the barriers going up, and he ground his teeth together in frustration. 'Have you any idea how crazy that sounds? Most women would want to know a man loves them and wants to marry them.'

Kari folded her arms around herself protectively. 'I'm not like most women.'

Through all the emotional upset, that made him smile faintly. 'No, you're not. That's why I love you and not someone else.'

Her throat closed over. 'Don't love me, Lance,' she advised gruffly, but he merely shook his head.

'Sorry, princess, but it's a done deal. Whilst there's a breath in my body, I'm going to go on loving you. I can't stop just because you don't want to love me,' he declared softly. 'I've waited my whole life for you, sweetheart, and I'm not going to let you go without a fight.'

Panic fluttered in her chest. 'You'll be wasting your time. There can never be anything between us.'

Lance picked up his shirt and shrugged it on, leaving the buttons unfastened. With a sigh he crossed to her, reaching out to brush a finger down one ashen cheek. 'Kari, you and I could be on opposite sides of the world and there would still be something between us. Time and distance have no meaning here. We love each other, whether you admit it or not.'

Kari felt the hot sting of tears in her eyes as she swayed back away from his touch. 'No. You're wrong. It's over, Lance. Just accept it,' she commanded coldly.

Accept it? Never! Quick as a flash, his hand snaked round her neck, drawing her head forward to meet his descending one. His kiss was hard, demanding a response which she tried so hard to deny him. But his lips and tongue wreaked havoc with her senses, and before she knew it she was kissing him back with a desperate hunger. When he released her mere seconds later, his grey eyes flared with triumph.

'Now tell me it's over,' he charged thickly, and because she had no answer she turned her head away.

'Get out!' she ordered shakily, and Lance sighed heavily before pressing a final kiss on her forehead and stepping back.

'I'll go, but this isn't over. I'll be back. You can count on it,' he promised hotly. Gathering up the rest of his things, he headed for the door. There, he turned and gave her one last look. 'I mean it. I'm not giving up, princess,' he warned before vanishing through the door and clattering down the stairs.

Sitting in his car, Lance stared up at the bedroom window. He meant it when he said it wasn't over. He couldn't walk away from her, not when he knew she loved him. Somehow he was going to make her tell him why the thought of loving him made her so afraid. That was the key to everything. Sighing, he reached for the ignition.

Kari didn't move until she heard his car engine fade into the distance, then she collapsed onto the bed and dropped her head in her hands. Two tears, all she would allow herself to shed, ran slowly down her cheeks.

She hurt, but it was nothing like the pain she knew she would feel if she allowed herself to care for Lance. Better a little heartache now than the harrowing pain she had gone through when she had lost Russ. She might have been foolish enough to fall in love with Lance, but she would fall out of love just as quickly. All she had to do was harden her heart against him. When he realised there was nothing for him here, that she had nothing to give him, he would let her go. And it would be for the best. He would come to realise it in the end.

With a heavy sigh, she stood up. Her heart twisted as she stared at the tangled bed sheets. She knew she could not sleep on them tonight for they carried his scent. Quickly she stripped the bed, carrying the dirty linen into the bathroom and shoving it into the laundry basket. Then she slipped out of the robe and stepped into the shower, standing under the stinging spray until the water began to cool.

Remaking the bed took all of her energy, and even her bones felt tired as she padded round the silent house, locking up. The day which had started so brightly had ended in a nightmare. When she finally crept into bed, she was exhausted, but as she lay staring up at the ceiling she knew that tonight, and for many nights to come, sleep would be a stranger.

CHAPTER EIGHT

LANCE slammed the phone down hard enough to break it. Damn the infuriating woman! She was refusing to take his calls.

Nick watched sombrely as his cousin paced back and forth across his office. 'She's one stubborn lady,' he observed mildly. He knew better than to joke. He had tried it once since Lance had told him what had happened, and narrowly missed being knocked into the middle of next week.

'I can be just as stubborn,' Lance responded forcefully. The trouble was, he was running out of time, and she knew it. He guessed she must be counting on it.

'You don't think you could have misjudged the situation?' Nick dared to ask, then held his hands up quickly when Lance sent a chilling glare his way. 'OK, OK. Don't jump down my throat. I get the message. She loves you.'

On the other side of the room, Lance sighed, rolling his neck to ease out the knots created during the better part of two frustrating days. Kari was nothing if not determined. He had tried calling at her house, but she had simply refused to answer the door. When a neighbour had threatened to call the police if he didn't stop making such a racket, he had been forced to withdraw. Telephone calls were worse. If she heard his voice, she hung up immediately. It was driving him crazy. He could not get through to her, and he didn't have the time to settle in for a siege. He had to catch the eight-thirty flight tonight.

It galled him to leave the matter unresolved. He knew if he did nothing she would strengthen her defences against him. He didn't want that. His best chance was to catch her whilst she was still vulnerable.

'Have you spoken to the Maitlands? If anyone can tell you about Kari, it's them.'

Nick's suggestion brought Lance's head round quickly. 'Of course. Why didn't I think of them?' he exclaimed, suddenly seeing a way of understanding what was happening. The Maitlands were exactly the people he needed to talk to. They alone could shed light on what made Kari tick. He glanced at his watch. It would be cutting it fine, but if he left now he would have just enough time to visit the Maitlands before he had to leave for the airport. 'Can I use the phone?'

'You know, you're going to get me fired,' Nick complained dryly, waving a hand towards the telephone.

'Good. It's the best thing that could happen to you,' Lance shot back bluntly, punching out the numbers.

Forty-five nerve-racking minutes later, he was once more in the Maitland house. Unable to relax, he paced back and forth before the fireplace in the lounge, whilst Robert and Georgia exchanged worried looks.

'You said it was urgent,' Robert prompted his young friend, and Lance took a deep steadying breath.

'You have to tell me about Kari,' he declared without preamble.

'Tell you what about her?' Georgia asked cautiously, though from Lance's agitation, and the signs of tiredness and strain on his face, she thought she could guess. Oh, dear.

'She refuses to marry me,' he responded tautly, and once again the older couple exchanged knowing looks.

'Perhaps she doesn't love you, son,' Robert suggested gently, and was more than a little amused to receive an impatient look for his pains.

'That's the one thing I am sure of in this whole sorry mess. She never said she didn't love me, just that she wouldn't love me. She refuses to, and won't tell me why.' The helplessness he had felt then returned now, and his jaw flexed tensely. 'I need to know what I'm fighting here. I know it must seem odd, my coming to you for help when it's your son's widow we're talking about, but there's nobody else for me to turn to. I love her. I won't give her up without a damn good fight,' he added forcefully.

It was Georgia who replied. 'We're glad you thought you could come to us. We love Kari, as much as if she were our own daughter. We want her to be happy, and if being with you would do that, then we would gladly give both of you our blessing. As for why she refuses to love you...Kari is a woman who loves without reservation, and that means any pain is equally deep. She was hurt very badly by Russ's death. I've never seen anyone in so much pain. You never knew her before. She was so free, so open. Loving and giving. When our son died, she closed herself off from love because it hurt too much. She believes that if she doesn't love anyone, then she cannot ever be hurt again.'

Her husband nodded solemnly. 'She gave up her horses because they reminded her of the pain.'

Lance dropped into the nearest chair and dragged his hands through his hair, seeing everything so clearly now. 'Why didn't she tell me that? I can understand her being afraid, but I know I can convince her she doesn't have to be. The trouble is, she refuses to see me or even speak to me.' He knew why, now. She was afraid he could persuade her, and that was too great a risk. He looked up then, his expression grave. 'Will you help me? I need to get her somewhere she can't run away, so that we can talk.'

Robert cleared his throat. 'Well, now, son, that's asking a great deal,' he said gruffly, and Georgia nodded her agreement.

'It isn't that we don't appreciate what you're saying, but we simply cannot hand her over to you without seeing for ourselves that it would be best for her. Hard as it may be for you to accept, Kari has the right to refuse you, Lance.'

Lance's jaw flexed as a wave of disappointment hit him. 'So you won't help me?'

'Now, now, we didn't say that,' Robert soothed with a smile.

'Indeed not,' Georgia confirmed. 'If you can curb

your totally natural impatience for a short while, we'll sound Kari out. Oh, we won't say anything about this visit, but it would ease my mind to be able to talk to her and find out what her feelings are for you. She's coming to dinner on Friday, and I'll have a quiet chat with her. Don't despair, Lance, we'll do our best for you.'

Lance knew that that was the best he could hope for. At least he could leave knowing someone would be fighting his corner for him. 'I appreciate it, believe me,' he responded, rising to his feet.

'Won't you stay for dinner?' Georgia urged in her motherly way.

'I would love to, but I'm afraid I can't. I'm booked on the eight-thirty flight to Denver,' Lance explained, glancing at his watch and knowing it was going to be nip and tuck to get to the airport in time. 'I have to go, but you can get hold of me through my office. Thank you for listening. I know Kari has first call on your loyalty.'

'She does,' Georgia agreed as they accompanied him to the door. 'But we'll help if we can. If we think it's right, we'll arrange for you to talk to her, but after that it's up to her. Now, drive carefully. There's always another flight. It wouldn't do your cause any good to end up in hospital, you know,' she advised him.

'I'll take it easy,' Lance promised, kissing her cheek. With a wave, he hurried down the steps to his car. The Maitlands watched him go.

'You realise he'd be perfect for her,' Robert murmured gently, putting an arm around his wife's shoulders.

'I know,' she sighed. 'But she's so afraid, Robert. So afraid.'

Kari tensed as the telephone issued its urgent summons, eyeing it as if it were some malevolent being. Her heart thumped anxiously for she knew who would be calling her. Lance had been gone two weeks now, but he called her regularly at the shop every morning. She had stopped answering the phone at home, but he left messages on her answer machine instead. He sent flowers, too. She had tried throwing them away once, but had rescued them from the trash almost immediately, unable to treat such inoffensive and beautiful things so badly. The latest bunch sat on her kitchen table, a constant reminder of him.

She knew what he was doing. He was making sure she could not forget him, and it was working. Not that she really needed the extra reminders. She missed him so much it was a constant ache inside her. She had thought that if she refused to love him, she wouldn't hurt, but she had been wrong. She was hurting. Hurting badly.

The ringing stopped as Jenny picked up the receiver. She listened for a moment then turned to her employer. 'It's Lance. Do you want to speak to him?' she asked, following a routine that she found increasingly frustrating.

Kari shook her head. 'No' she refused unevenly, picking up an invoice and struggling to get it into focus. Why wouldn't he just leave her alone?

'I'm sorry, Lance,' she heard Jenny say softly. 'OK, I will... Goodbye.' The receiver went back down, and when she glanced up Jenny was shaking her head. Instantly Kari's nerves leapt.

'Is something wrong?' she demanded anxiously, and her assistant looked at her helplessly.

'No, but if you're concerned, you could always talk to him,' Jenny suggested, sighing when predictably Kari turned away, pretending an interest in her paperwork.

'I have nothing to say to him.' She didn't want to hear his voice, for it stirred up feelings she was determined to conquer.

'Well, in case you're interested, Lance said to tell you he loves you very much, and that you were to take care of yourself,' Jenny repeated gently. 'He really cares about you, you know,' she added for the nth time, knowing it was bound to fail, but needing to say something to end this stalemate between two people she liked and respected.

'I know you mean well, Jenny, but there are things you don't understand,' Kari responded tiredly.

'You're right,' Jenny snapped. 'I don't understand why you won't even talk to him. How many times does the man have to tell you he loves you before you forgive him?' she added, knowing she was being unfair, but unable to help herself. It was just so wrong. 'I used to think you were made for each other. Now I'm beginning to think you don't deserve him!' she finished and stomped out of the office before Kari could respond.

Kari closed her eyes. 'We're not made for each

other,' she whispered painfully to the closed door, though deep in her heart she knew it was true. They had fitted together like two halves of a whole. For anyone else it would have been perfect, but for her it was unbearable. If only he didn't keep telling her he loved her. She might have stood some chance of forgetting him. The words were a knife in her heart. Another wound that would take a long time to heal.

To cap it all she was having bad dreams again. In the days and months after Russ had died, she had experienced them constantly. Over the years they had lessened until she had believed them gone for good. These last few nights had proved her wrong, and they were as powerful now as they had ever been.

As had become her habit she worked late that evening, hoping to tire herself out enough to ward off the inevitable dream. Dinner was a slice of cold pizza she could barely swallow. She ate watching an old black-and-white movie but she couldn't have told anyone what it was about the second after she switched the TV off.

Reluctantly she was forced into her bed, praying that tonight would be different, but the dream came snaking into her subconscious when her defences were at their lowest. It always started the same way. She was in the stable, grooming the horses, when she experienced a stark sense of danger coming at her from behind.

She wanted to run. Run as fast as she could. Yet though she tried they caught her. She fought, but couldn't break free. She was dragged back by hands that hurt her. She was trapped and couldn't breathe.

There was something over her mouth making it impossible for her to cry out. A man's hand. Now she couldn't move. There was a weight on her, pressing her down, down. A man's body. A whimper left her throat.

Then she heard Russ calling her name. He was coming closer and she desperately wanted to stop him, because she knew what would happen. If she could only stop him he would be safe, but she couldn't call out. And then she saw the gun and knew it was too late. Her head was filled with the sound of the explosion, and at last she could scream…no…no…

'No-o!'

The anguished cry brought Kari awake with painful suddenness. She was sitting up in her bed, drenched in sweat, the covers twisted around her like winding-sheets. Her heart pounded sickeningly fast in her chest.

'Oh, God,' she sighed, the words a despairing croak.

She knew the nightmare had returned because she was feeling especially vulnerable. She had made the mistake of getting too close to Lance, and it had resurrected her fears. Those fears had resurrected the nightmare. Reliving the past in her dreams was all the proof she needed to convince her she couldn't risk her heart again.

She was doing the right thing. The only thing. If only it didn't hurt so much.

The following evening she went to dinner with the Maitlands. She usually dined with them once a week,

but last Friday she had had to beg off due to a really
bad headache. Tonight, though she was bone tired
from lack of sleep, she knew she could do with the
company of people whose caring was undemanding.

Conversation was light through dinner, and neither
Robert nor Georgia made any comment when she
occasionally drifted into her own thoughts. As the
evening went on she found herself relaxing just a
little. They had coffee on the terrace, and later she
and her mother-in-law walked in the garden whilst
her father-in-law remained behind puffing on a cigar.

'You're looking tired, dear. Aren't you sleeping
well?' Georgia asked in some concern. This was the
first time she had seen for herself the effect of Kari's
broken relationship with Lance.

Kari thought about lying, but she needed to talk
to someone. 'The dreams are back,' she confessed,
and Georgia caught her breath sharply.

'Oh, no, Kari! I thought they were gone for good.
What's brought them back, do you know?' Of
course, Georgia knew full well, but she needed Kari
to tell her herself.

Kari folded her arms, rubbing her hands over her
upper arms as if she were chilled. 'Lance. It's Lance.
I'd…been seeing him, you see. I had no idea he felt
so…strongly,' she explained, swallowing a painful
lump in her throat. 'I didn't set out to make him love
me. Now he wants to marry me!'

Georgia came to a halt, picking up a dead head
off a rose and tucking it in her pocket. 'And you?'
she asked, as if it were a matter of no great impor-

tance. 'How do you feel about him?'

Kari pressed her lips together to still their tendency to tremble. 'I don't want to love him!' she exclaimed passionately, bringing the merest twist of a sad smile to her mother-in-law's mouth. Lance was right. Her daughter-in-law was fighting her feelings, but she loved him. Loved him deeply.

'It seems to me you don't have much choice, dear. If you love him, and it sounds as if you do, then surely as he loves you the logical thing would be to marry him,' she said sensibly, turning away from the roses and raising her eyebrows in gentle query.

Kari chewed on her lip. 'I daren't,' she replied in a choked voice.

'But you've thought about it?'

She had. Though she had done her best not to, it had proved impossible not to wonder, What if? But the memories would return, bringing the cloying fear with it. 'I can't go through it all again!' she exclaimed emotionally. 'How could he expect me to?'

'*Does* he expect you to? Does he know why you won't marry him?' Georgia asked curiously, and Kari looked away.

'No,' she admitted reluctantly, and Georgia slipped a hand through her arm and urged her to walk on.

'Don't you think that's being a little unfair? Expecting him to accept a refusal without telling him why?'

'He'll try to persuade me to change my mind. I know he will!'

Georgia bit back a smile. 'But if your mind is made up, what difference will that make?' she argued reasonably. It should have none, unless, secretly, Kari hoped he would succeed. Which, given her state of mind, was entirely possible.

'I just want him to stop pestering me,' Kari declared frustratedly. 'He calls, and sends me flowers. He's driving me insane! I have to get away for a while, Mother, until Lance accepts that I mean what I say. But where can I go?'

Georgia made an instant decision, knowing Robert would agree with her. 'Well, now, perhaps I can help you. It just so happens an old colleague of Robert's was saying only the other day that he had a library in dire need of cataloguing. I know you've done a similar thing before, so this would be right up your street. I'm sure he would jump at the chance of having you do it, and it would kill two birds with one stone. What do you think?'

Kari didn't have to think. She realised it could be her salvation. It might help put some distance between her and Lance, something she needed badly in order to regain her equilibrium. 'Of course I'll do it. Jenny is quite capable of looking after the shop, so I don't have to worry about that. It would be perfect.'

'That's settled, then. I shall get Robert to arrange it,' Georgia declared brightly, satisfied in her own mind that she was doing the right thing. Now she wisely changed the subject. 'Come and tell me what you think of my zinnias.'

Later, when Kari had gone home, she sought out her husband who was getting ready for bed. 'I'm going to give Lance a call in the morning,' she told him in her no-nonsense way, and he looked at her with a twinkle in his eye.

'You're that certain, are you?'

Georgia nodded, feeling very much like crying. 'I shall miss her, but she loves Lance. She just needs to be persuaded to stop being so afraid. Lance is the only one who can do it. I think he deserves the chance to try, at least.'

'You're a very perceptive woman, Georgia, and I trust your instincts. Come and give your old reprobate a hug. I think I'm feeling just a little blue tonight,' he murmured, taking her in his arms, knowing their life was going to change once more, but at least this time for the better.

Two days later, Kari was on a plane heading west. The details had been arranged in remarkably short time, but that didn't bother her. The sooner the better, as far as she was concerned. Jenny had a number to call in the event of emergencies, but Kari had made her swear that under no circumstances would she give it to Lance.

The first leg of her trip was unexpectedly luxurious. Jack and Rachel Gaines, the owners of the library, had insisted on paying for her flight, and Kari was rather bemused to find herself travelling first class. She knew from her instructions that she would have to change planes twice, the planes getting progressively smaller, and that somebody would be there to meet her at her final destination to drive her to the house.

The last leg of the trip was as a passenger on a small plane delivering freight. It gave her her only clue that her destination was not a major airport, but she had not expected to end the journey at a landing-strip in the middle of nowhere, with the only building in sight an old barn. The pilot saw nothing odd in it though, for, after helping her down, he immediately began unloading several boxes along with her bags, stacking them in the shade of the barn.

When he was done, he turned to her with a friendly smile. 'Somebody ought to be along to fetch you any time now, ma'am. Fact, that'll be them now, I reckon.' Kari followed his pointing arm and noticed a plume of dust in the distance. 'You have a nice day now,' he added with a tip of his hat, and climbed back into his plane. Waving his hand, he taxied back out to the end of the runway, and in minutes was airborne again.

Kari had no option but to turn her attention to the dust which was definitely getting closer. It took nearly ten minutes for the vehicle to come into view, and several more before what turned out to be a truck came to a halt and a tall figure climbed out and began walking towards her.

He was wearing a hat, and his face was in shadow, yet there was something in the purposeful easy stride which looked awfully familiar. He came a little closer and her mouth went dry. Heart thumping, she stood frozen in disbelief. It was Lance. The man walking towards her, despite the scuffed boots, faded denims and pale blue shirt, was Lance Kersee. The very man she had come here to avoid.

'Sorry I'm late, princess,' Lance apologised smoothly. Damn, but he was pleased to see her. He wanted to haul her into his arms and never let her go. These past few weeks had been hell, but she was here now, and she wouldn't be able to avoid him again. As he neared her he ran a careful eye over her, seeing the underlying weariness. She had chosen a hard row to harrow, and it was beginning to tell on her. 'The truck blew a tyre and I had to stop and change it. Just give me a few minutes to load this stuff, and we'll be on our way.'

Dumbstruck, she watched him heft the boxes into the back of the truck. One thing was suddenly crystal clear: his presence here was no accident. A trap had been set, and she had walked into it. Moreover, it had been done with the connivance of people she loved and trusted. Her sense of betrayal was immense, and anger began to simmer inside her as she waited for him to finish. She didn't know how he had prevailed upon the Maitlands to help him, but if he thought she was simply going to accept it, he was mistaken.

Lance didn't look at her, but he could feel the animosity coming off her in waves as he picked up her bags. Bracing himself mentally, he dusted off his hands nonchalantly and turned to her again. 'That's it. Time to go.'

She didn't budge an inch. 'What are you doing here, Lance?' she demanded angrily.

He quirked an eyebrow at her, smiling faintly. 'Collecting you, as arranged,' he replied coolly, knowing her wrath was about to crash down on him, but anything was better than the silence he had been getting.

Kari stared at him coldly, so furious she felt like throwing something at him. 'I suppose you think you've been very clever!' she exclaimed scathingly. 'You and your accomplices.'

'Robert and Georgia have your best interests at heart.'

She had thought so too, but after this she wasn't so sure. 'Really? I doubt it, or they wouldn't have set me up like this. By the way, who exactly are the Gaineses?'

'Rachel is my sister. Jack is her husband,' he informed her calmly.

'Well, at least you kept it in the family!' she retorted waspishly. 'Damn it, you had no right to do this!'

His smile vanished and he took a step towards her. 'Do you think I wanted it this way? You forced me to it, Kari, when you refused to talk to me. I told you I wouldn't give up.'

He had, she just hadn't imagined he would go to such lengths. Nor, she added bitterly, that he would have help. 'I'll never forgive any of you for this!' she declared tautly.

That was the one thing Lance was the most afraid of, but it was too late now, the die was cast. 'I'll take my chances,' he responded, managing to sound unconcerned. 'We'd better get going. It will take us a while to get back to the house.'

Kari shook her head, standing her ground. 'I'm not

going anywhere with you. I'm going to take the next plane home,' she declared coldly.

Lance tipped his hat back on his head and hooked his hands on his hips, taking his weight on one leg in an attitude so typically male, her stomach clenched involuntarily. 'You'll have a long wait. Nothing stops here unless it's arranged.'

Her eyes narrowed. He was being deliberately obtuse. 'I meant from the airport. I expect you to take me there,' she ground out impatiently.

'Sorry, princess, but you aren't going anywhere except to the house. Rachel has a room all made up for you.'

Kari stared at him in disbelief. 'That's kidnapping!' she exclaimed angrily, but he merely shrugged.

'Call it what you like. Now, are you going to get into the truck or am I going to have to put you in?' he challenged.

She stiffened in outrage. 'Lay one finger on me, and I swear I'll kill you!' she threatened, holding up a hand to ward him off in case he should try it. She knew he would make good his threat and that was unthinkable. Loath as she was, she knew she had to go with him. But only as far as the nearest town where she could hire a car. She was not going to stay here. She absolutely was not!

'All right, I'll come, but I'll despise you for ever,' she told him witheringly, stomping past him to climb up into the passenger seat, slamming the door behind her and sitting staring rigidly ahead. Shaking with anger, she waited for him to join her.

With a soundless whistle Lance took his seat, started the engine and swung the truck round onto the track which led to the house. Kari religiously studied the view out the window. She had no idea where they were, except somewhere in Wyoming. She regretted not looking the address up on the map, but she had been in too much of a hurry to get away. Not that it would have helped much, but at least she would have known how far away the nearest town was.

'Your jaw will break if you keep clenching it that hard,' he observed dryly, and Kari looked round at him glacially but said nothing. 'Are you going to ignore me the whole trip?'

'Sounds good to me,' she returned frostily.

Lance hid a grin. Hate him she might, but ignore him she couldn't. 'I regret having to do this, you know. It goes against the grain, but I'm a desperate man, princess, willing to do desperate things in order not to lose you,' he admitted conversationally, manoeuvring the truck around a series of potholes, trying to keep the vehicle from bouncing around too much.

Kari angled her head just enough to be able to study him without appearing to do so. He looked a little ragged around the edges. Like a man who had not slept well for some time. Her heart contracted, for she knew the feeling. But that didn't excuse him. He had gone too far.

'So you thought you'd try a little kidnapping,' she derided. 'What happens when that doesn't work? For it won't, you know.'

Lance couldn't allow himself to think in terms of failure. This had to succeed. 'All I want you to do is talk to me, princess. Help me to understand why this has to end,' he said reasonably. 'Telling me not to love you is like telling the earth to stop spinning—downright impossible.'

She had no smart comeback to that, for she knew her own feelings hadn't changed either. She hadn't wanted to care for him, yet that had made no difference. But falling in love with him had been a mistake, and she wasn't going to compound it by allowing the relationship to develop any further than it had. There was no point in talking. She had to harden her heart and remain firm.

'Then forget me instead. It's the same thing.'

Lance looked away from the track long enough to smile into her eyes. 'You're unforgettable, princess. Don't you know that?'

Kari averted her eyes, swallowing a lump which had suddenly formed in her throat. He was unforgettable too. Scarcely a minute had gone by without her thinking of him, longing for his warmth and strength. His love. Everything seemed so colourless without him. Lance was the source of all her happiness and her despair. He was all she ever wanted, but she couldn't allow herself to have him, for if she lost him too she would never recover from the pain of it. How could anyone expect her to risk that? She'd have to be insane to do so—wouldn't she?

'How far is it to your sister's house?' she asked abruptly, needing to distract her thoughts from the unexpected line they were taking. They had driven

miles and still no house was in sight. She didn't
know how long she could stand being this close to
him. His nearness was making her nerves tingle.

'About another fifteen minutes or so. The landing-
strip is the nearest level piece of ground to the house.
The ranch house is actually nestled into those hills
up ahead of us.' Lance nodded to the high ground
which was getting closer by the minute.

She looked around her in surprise. The spread had
to be enormous. 'I had no idea this was a ranch. I
don't see any cattle,' she murmured, forgetting her
anger in her curiosity.

Lance tensed a little as he answered. 'That's because it isn't a cattle ranch any longer. Jack breeds
horses. He has one of the finest studs in the country.'
He knew he had just dropped quite a bombshell, and
wondered how she would take it.

Kari felt as if she had been hit in the stomach.
'Horses?' she checked, hoping she had misheard but
knowing she hadn't. Her skin suddenly felt prickly.
She hadn't been near a horse since Russ died. Had
been too afraid.

Lance cast her an assessing glance before pressing
on relentlessly. She had to face her devils in order
to conquer them. 'Do you ride?'

She shivered a little. 'I used to.'

'We'll go for a ride whilst you're here, let you see
something of the country,' he suggested easily, and
Kari frowned.

'I don't ride any more,' she said repressively, hoping he would drop the subject. Predictably, he didn't.

'Why not?' he probed, wondering if she would tell him.

Because in her mind horses were inextricably linked with remembered pain. 'I just got out of the habit,' she murmured evasively.

Lance sighed but knew it was unreasonable to expect her to tell him so soon. It was going to take time, but that was something they had plenty of right now. When he had taken Georgia's call he had felt hope for the first time in weeks. It had taken very little persuasion to get his sister to help, especially when he'd told her he had arranged for her to join Jack for a long-awaited vacation. Jack had been off delivering horses down south, but instead of his coming home Rachel was flying down to join him. He and Kari would have the place to themselves.

The house was coming into view. Kari had expected to see Rachel Gaines standing out on the porch to greet them, but the place looked deserted. An uneasy feeling crept over her.

'Where's your other accomplice?' she asked edgily as they pulled up outside, hoping he wouldn't say what she was dreading he might.

'Rachel is on her way to join her husband. You have me all to yourself, princess,' he told her sardonically, confirming her suspicions.

'I'd rather share a hole with a snake!' she snapped, and Lance threw back his head and laughed. At the sound her heart turned over. Though she hated herself for doing it, she was unable to stop her eyes eating him up. She had missed him so very much, even though she had tried not to. She should be angry

with him. *Was* angry but her heart wasn't listening
to her head. It only knew that she had missed him.

Shaking his head, Lance climbed out of the truck.
About to do likewise, Kari caught sight of the key
dangling in the ignition. Her nerves leapt. He had
forgotten the keys! But, even as the prospect of escape arose, Lance reached in and removed the key.
Her eyes followed the movement as he slipped it into
the pocket of his jeans.

'Just in case you get the urge to slip out in the
night and make a bolt for it,' he drawled mockingly,
and her eyes met his laughing ones.

Kari saw her escape route cut off in its prime. 'Did
I ever tell you how loathsome you are?' she exclaimed in frustration, and he smiled.

'I seem to recall you mentioning it once or twice.'

She turned her back on him and jumped down.
Flapping inadequately at the dust which had settled
on her during the long drive, she studied the house
grudgingly. She didn't want to like anything about
the place, but there was no denying it was beautiful.
Old and weathered, it had a grandeur that was needed
in a country that could make a person feel very small
and insignificant.

'Is there really a library here?' she asked dryly.
'Or did you make that up too?'

Lance reached into the back of the truck for her
bags. 'Oh, no. Jack's great-great-grandfather started
it, and every generation since has added to it. It's
huge and in desperate need of cataloguing. You'll
love it.'

'Don't imagine for one second that my love of

books will make me accept being here against my will. If I get the chance, I'll leave,' she told him forthrightly.

Lance held her bags in one hand and used the other to take her by the arm and steer her towards the porch. 'I wouldn't advise attempting it on foot. The nearest property is several days' walk away, even if you know which direction to take. Added to which, we get snakes out here,' he cautioned.

Kari launched one of those incomparable looks at him, designed to pin him to the spot. 'There are snakes everywhere, and in my considered opinion the two-legged variety are the worst!' she said pithily, and swept into the house pursued by another burst of laughter.

CHAPTER NINE

KARI stirred and rolled over in the bed, opening her eyes slowly. Dappled sunlight filtered into the room, and she watched dust motes dancing in the faint breeze from the window. The house lay silent around her, but she had no idea if it was early or late. All she could hear was the melodic calls of the birds.

As she lay there unwilling to move, she realised that it was the first time she had slept through the night in weeks. In fact, not since she had last slept in Lance's arms had she slept so dreamlessly. Her heart twisted. It would be simple to say it had been due to the exhaustion of travel, but she would be lying. She knew it was because Lance had been in the same house. Her subconscious had accepted something her waking mind could not—that he brought her a measure of peace nothing else did. Which was so confusing, when the thought of loving him scared her so much.

She sighed and stretched, then stilled as another sound reached her ears. She knew it at once. Not far away, horses were whinnying to each other. She tried to ignore it, but the sound was a siren call tugging at her heart, and it drew her out of the bed and across to the window. The house was surrounded by paddocks, and there were small groups of horses dotted about them. Even at that distance she could see them tossing their heads, shaking out the kinks left over from the night.

It brought a smile to her lips, which surprised her a little, for she hadn't been able to take pleasure from horses in such a long time. Frowning, she stepped back. Why was everything so contrary all of a sudden? First she slept when she shouldn't have, and now she was thinking of horses with pleasure. It unsettled her. She had always known what she had to do, but it was as if the edges were blurring. She could no longer be quite sure what was for the best and what wasn't.

Unsettled, and disliking it, she picked up her watch and discovered it was getting on for ten o'clock. She had slept for hours. Her first instinct was to be angry that Lance hadn't woken her up, but then she realised how much better she felt for the rest. OK, he had done the right thing, but that didn't mean she was any less angry with him for shanghaiing her. Showering quickly, she dressed in jeans and a T-shirt and went downstairs.

The kitchen was empty, but there were signs Lance had been there from the dishes on the drainer. She helped herself to some juice from the refrigerator, and sipped at it whilst she made herself some toast. She was just finishing it when Lance walked in.

The impact of him hit her with the force of a thunderbolt. He smelled of horses and fresh air, and the jeans and shirt he wore made him look so ruggedly sexy, her body went molten. She remembered how he felt, how he tasted, and her senses craved him in the worst way. Her breathing grew ragged, and she knew if she had been standing her legs would have failed her.

Lance knew exactly how she was feeling, because he was experiencing the same thing. This attraction between them was a pretty powerful thing. Her eyes... They aroused a need in him that almost made him groan out loud. His body reacted, surging against his jeans, and he knew if her gaze dropped he would damn well explode. Needing to distract himself, he walked painfully to the sink and drew himself a glass of water. Only when he was moderately sure he had himself under control did he clear his throat and turn to her.

'Sleep well, princess?'

Kari had been relieved when he'd stopped looking at her. The look in his eyes had nearly sent her up in flames. 'You should have woken me earlier,' she complained snappily.

Lance rested back against the sink and crossed his feet. 'You looked too peaceful. I hadn't the heart to do it.'

It took a second or two for the meaning to reach her, then her eyes rounded accusingly. 'You were in my room?' she gasped in outrage.

'I came to ask you if you wanted to go riding,' he explained with a shrug. But as he had bent over her he had seen the bruises under her eyes, and known she needed sleep more than he needed explanations right then. He had gone out again without disturbing her.

Her back stiffened. 'I told you, I don't ride,' she said frostily, and he smiled wryly.

'I know you did, sugar, but I figured there was no harm in asking. You might have changed your mind.'

'I won't,' she insisted.

'We'll see,' he countered, and she was tempted to throw something at the maddening man. Realising her temper was on a short rein, Lance pushed himself upright. 'You ready to see the library?' he asked, diverting her.

Kari took a calming breath before rising. 'Yes, I am.'

Lance walked to the door leading to the rest of the house and held it open for her. 'Then follow me, princess, and I'll show you your heart's delight.'

He wasn't far wrong. The library was a book lover's dream. Floor-to-ceiling shelves were crammed with volumes of all shapes and descriptions. There were even, she noted in amazement, a couple of Biedermeier bookcases set between the windows, which even at a brief glance she could see held several first editions. Like a kid in a sweet shop, she looked about her in awe. This was like having all her Christmases at once.

'Incredible!' she breathed, her eyes alight with expectation.

Lance grinned at her reaction. 'Thought you'd be impressed,' he remarked fondly, and she so far forgot herself as to smile at him.

'I am. Very.'

'Good. That's what I hoped you would say,' he responded, walking to where a computer sat on a library table at one end of the large room. 'Rachel had this brought in for you. There's a cataloguing program already installed, from when she had the idea of doing it herself. Think you can make use of it?'

Kari felt dazed. 'Yes. Of course. It's…overwhelming.' She picked out a book at random from the nearest shelf and was lost in it in seconds.

'I'll leave you to it, then,' Lance murmured wryly, and when she made no reply he accepted she was lost to him for the time being and left her there.

Kari looked up some time later, shrugging when she realised she was alone. She wasted half a second wondering where he had gone, before the task at hand caught her interest. She spent the whole day there, as happy as Larry, not even emerging for lunch. Lance brought her a sandwich and a glass of milk, but she barely stopped long enough to thank him.

Time passed, but she had no recollection of it, and looked up in surprise when Lance reappeared beside her again.

He didn't know whether to be angry or amused. Her pristine white T-shirt was smudged with dust and grime, and she even had smudges on her cheek where she must have brushed her hair back. Yet she looked happy, and he realised she hadn't really been hiding away from him, but had been so caught up in what she was dong she had no sense of time. He, on the other hand, had felt every second of her absence like an ache in his chest. He could, he knew, become just a little jealous of all these books she handled so lovingly.

'OK, that's it,' he declared purposefully, taking the book she had been reading out of her hands and closing it. 'Save whatever you have on the computer and shut it down. You've just got time to wash up before supper.'

'Supper?' She blinked at him.

He felt like a father with his child. 'Yes. You remember. It's that meal which comes between lunch and breakfast.'

Her eyes narrowed at that. 'Don't be funny!' she retorted, suddenly aware of how stiff her back was. She stretched painfully. 'Ouch. I seem to have lost track of time,' she muttered, wincing again as her muscles protested.

'You don't say,' he drawled sardonically, watching her shut the computer down and put the desk to rights. Then he pulled back her chair and helped her to her feet, pointing her towards the door. 'Go. The books will still be here tomorrow. Wash your hands like a good little librarian, and don't forget your face!' he directed, giving her a tiny shove.

She shrugged him off, but only half-heartedly. 'Stop giving me orders!' she growled, but headed for the door all the same.

Lance followed close behind. 'I've got steak and salad waiting on the table, and there's a bottle of wine cooling in the refrigerator. If you're not down in five minutes, I'm giving yours to the dog,' he told her as he walked round her and disappeared down the hall to the kitchen.

Kari poked her tongue at his back, but as she climbed the stairs she could smell the delicious aroma of fried steak and her mouth started watering. Only then did she realise how hungry she was. It added a spring to her step as she hurried up to her room. She was back down again in a little over five minutes, washed and dressed in a clean blouse. Lance was just pouring out the wine when she joined him.

'Just made it,' he said, glancing at his watch.

'Hmm, smells good,' Kari declared eagerly. She hadn't felt this hungry in weeks.

'It will taste even better. Go ahead, dig in,' he invited, and she didn't wait for more.

It wasn't until the edge had gone off her hunger, and she was on her second glass of wine, that Kari finally looked across the table at Lance and her brow creased in consternation. His purpose in bringing her here had been to get her to talk to him, yet he had left her alone all day. He hadn't pressured her in any way. He had given her the present of the library and gone away, leaving her to enjoy it on her own. It had been a selfless thing to do, and it thawed the ice she had been trying to form about her heart.

Sensing her gaze, Lance glanced up from his own plate and smiled. 'Feeling better?'

'Much.' She nodded, chewing at her lip. 'Why did you leave me alone all day?' she asked curiously.

Lance set his knife down and reached for his glass. 'Did you miss me?' he challenged with a glint in his eye.

'No,' she rejoined repressively, but he only

laughed. 'I thought you brought me here to talk,' she pointed out, and he shrugged easily.

'When you're ready, we'll talk.'

'What if I'm never ready?'

'You will be,' he countered confidently, causing her to frown again.

'How can you be so sure?'

Lance leant forward, his expression gentle. 'Because you love me, princess. Because you love me. Now, finish your food. You don't look as if you've been eating nearly enough.'

Kari looked down at her plate in confusion. There was no answering his arguments. No breaking his confidence. He was like the constant drip of water boring away at a stone. Everything he said made her feel less and less sure that her path was the right one. Yet it had to be—hadn't it? Only a fool would wilfully step back into the fire they had been burned in.

A fool—or someone with the guts to take a chance on happiness? A week ago she would have said the former, but now... Racked by uncertainty, she picked up her knife and fork and started eating again.

That day set the pattern for the next few. Lance was always up before her, and Kari would eat her breakfast with the sound of the horses' enticing calls echoing faintly on the breeze. She would then spend the day in the library, beavering away, until Lance came to tell her it was time for supper. They ate together, and he would tell her this and that about what he had been doing, making it sound so normal they could have been an old married couple.

As the days went slowly by, it began to dawn on her that she was forgetting to be afraid. Lance was still Lance, but her feelings for him didn't bother her half as much as they had done in the beginning. It was as if being with him had dulled her fears. They were still there, but they didn't haunt her quite so much.

Though she would occasionally sit out on the porch, she never went near the stables. She knew Lance went there every day, but she had not taken up any of his offers to go riding. Yet it was getting more difficult, because the presence of the horses was getting to her. Each morning she awoke to hear them calling, and she would stand at her window for a longer time, watching from a distance.

This morning was no different. As she stood there, the tug on her heart was more powerful than ever. Part of her longed to go to them. There was an emptiness inside her she knew only being with the animals she loved could fill. She was only half a person without them, and suddenly she realised how desperately she wanted to feel whole again. Cutting them out of her life had seemed the right thing to do, but now she admitted just how much she had missed them. Yet it didn't have to be that way any longer. She had the remedy. All she had to do was go out there. She stared out the window and wondered why she was still hesitating when she knew what she wanted.

The decision was made that easily, and, not wanting to give herself time to think, she turned away and reached for her clothes. When she was comfortably dressed in jeans and a light sweater, she slipped from her room and hurried down the stairs. Outside, she took a deep breath and headed off towards the nearest paddock.

Her steps slowed as she approached it, for she was suddenly caught between the past and the present. Yet the horses called to her, and they were the spur that took her the few feet to the fence. When she reached it, she rested her arms along the top rail and watched with a fierce glow of pleasure burning inside her. The horses were so beautiful. She knew they had sensed her presence from the angle of their heads, and, after the briefest hesitation, one turned and made its way towards her.

She tensed immediately, instinctively poised to retreat, but something stronger than fear held her there. Her heart was racing as she watched the proud animal approach, and then one velvety nose gently nudged at her arm. Emotion welled up inside her, blocking her throat. Pressing one hand to her trembling lips, she reached out with the other to stroke the silky head, waiting for the painful memories to hit her.

They didn't come. She blinked, testing again, but again there was no pain and probably hadn't been for some time. If she hadn't been so fearful she might have known it sooner, and she was filled with a deep sense of regret that she had denied herself this pleasure for so long for no reason.

'Lord, I've been such a fool,' she murmured softly, rubbing her cheek against the velvety smooth coat as tears of relief ran down her cheeks.

'Kari?'

Lance's soft query made her jump and spin round. Swallowing, she hastily rubbed at her eyes.

'Are you OK, honey?' he asked cautiously, not wanting to spook her.

He had been dressing when he had heard her slip quietly down the stairs and out of the house. From his window he had seen the direction she had taken, and it had galvanised him into action. He had thrown on his clothes haphazardly and followed her. Very much aware that this was the first time she had shown any interest in the horses, he had found a suitable vantage point to watch her from. Wanting to be on hand if she needed him.

His heart had twisted as he'd watched her reach out to the horse. He had known it was a special moment, and could make all the difference to their relationship. He had watched silently, scarcely breathing for fear of shattering the mood. For the shortest while he had thought it was going to be all right, and then she had shifted slightly, and he had seen the tears on her face. It had brought a fierce ache to his chest. She was hurting, and he had had to go to her.

Kari cleared her throat, embarrassed at being caught out this way. 'I'm fine,' she said in a voice made husky by tears.

Unable to stop himself, Lance reached across and wiped a lone drop of moisture from her cheek, rubbing it broodingly between his thumb and forefinger. 'I'm sorry. I didn't bring you here to make you cry,' he said regretfully, and Kari turned back to where the horse was patiently waiting.

'Don't be sorry. For this at least I'm glad I'm here. It's made me realise just how much I miss my horses. I should never have given them up.' She sighed.

Lance came to stand by her. 'Why did you?'

The truth came easily. 'Because when I needed them they couldn't comfort me, and I thought they would only ever give me pain. I was wrong,' she revealed sadly, then frowned as she considered another possibility. If she had been wrong about this, what else might she be wrong about?

'They reminded you of Russ?' Lance probed carefully, not wanting to stop her now that she was at last talking to him. The other horses had come up and he greeted them all in turn, though never taking his eyes off her.

Kari nodded, not surprised by his swift understanding. He seemed to know her better than she knew herself. Which should tell her something. Almost without thinking, she found herself talking. 'He died in our stable, you see.'

Lance tensed. He hadn't expected that. He had thought Russ Maitland must have died in a failed hold-up of some sort, not on their own property. He recalled her telling him she had been there, and he felt sick. Dear God, what else had happened? 'I...didn't know that,' he responded carefully.

Kari absently stroked the horse's neck, her thoughts in the past. 'He went out on a call, and I decided to walk over to the stable to see to the horses as it was such a warm day. The minute I stepped inside I knew something was wrong. The horses were very uneasy. I knew I ought to get out, but when I turned to leave there was a man between me and the door. Another came up behind me. Both had guns.' She shivered, remembering how trapped she had felt. How frightened.

Lance's hands curled into fists. He knew what was coming, and it was the very last thing he wanted to hear. The thought of her being hurt by those men made him want to hit something—hard. He took a reflexive step towards her, then forced himself to be still. 'Go on,' he urged tautly, bracing himself.

'One of them stood by whilst the other grabbed me. I didn't make it easy for him. I fought the best way I could, with my feet and my hands. I called him all the vile names I could think of, and he didn't like it. He hit me, and I was so dazed I couldn't stop him pushing me to the floor and tearing at my clothes. I remember thinking, Dear God, he's going to rape me, when I heard Russ's voice. He had finished early and come to find me. For one wild moment I thought I was saved, and then I realised just how much danger he was in, and how I could do nothing to stop him from walking into it...' Her voice tailed away at that point, and when she looked at him Lance could see the haunted expression in her eyes.

'They shot him?' he asked, though he knew it was unnecessary.

She nodded, swallowing to ease a painfully tight throat. 'As he came to help me. He never stood a chance. I saw him fall and I screamed. I'm not too clear on what happened then, because they knocked me out. When I came to, I was alone with Russ. He wasn't dead, not quite, but he had been shot more than once, and one bullet had caught him in the groin. There was blood everywhere, and I couldn't do anything to stop it, however much I tried. If I had had the car, I could have called for help, but it was back at the house and the men had taken Russ's. I knew he would be dead before I could get there and back.' Kari took a deep breath before going on. 'So I stayed and held him in my arms until he died. They were the longest five minutes of my life. He only had time to tell me he loved me, and then he was gone.'

Lance reached across and placed his hand on her shoulder, squeezing it gently. 'I'm sorry you had to go through that, princess,' he said thickly.

She looked at him sadly. 'Russ didn't deserve to die that way.'

'Nobody does, honey. Nobody does.'

Kari nodded, smiling her thanks at his understanding. The horse whickered, reminding her she had stopped stroking him, and her smile widened as she tugged at his ears. 'Am I ignoring you? Oh-h-h, you are so handsome. You know it too, don't you?' she laughed softly.

'Did they hurt you, Kari?' Lance queried tightly, bringing her attention back to him.

She knew what he was asking. Could see the pain in his eyes. She was glad she could ease it. 'They didn't rape me. Russ saved me from that,' she answered huskily, and he closed his eyes as relief made his head swim.

'Thank God,' he declared fervently, and the rage to commit murder faded. 'Who were they, do you know?'

Kari's expression tightened. 'Two men who had failed to rob a bank in the next county. They shot two people escaping, and ended up in our stable because it was the first building they came to after the car they stole ran out of gas. One was caught because he broke a leg when they crashed Russ's car. The other is still out there, no doubt ruining other lives,' she ended bitterly.

'They'll catch him one day.'

'I hope so,' she agreed, then sighed. 'So, now you know what happened. Why I stopped riding. I gave up my horses because I couldn't bear to love them with Russ gone. It felt better to lose them, too.' She grimaced self-consciously. 'It sounds a little crazy, but at the time I wasn't thinking very clearly. My husband was dead, and all the joy had gone out of my life.'

He guessed he would never know how she felt. All he could do was imagine life without her in it, and that was a possibility too awful to contemplate. 'And now?' he prompted, watching her greet the other horses with smiles and soft laughter.

Her smile, when she glanced his way, was almost shy. 'I'm getting it back.'

Lance was glad he had been able to return to her some of that lost joy. If only she would let him, he would gladly spend the rest of his life filling her life to the brim with joy and happiness. And that could start now.

'Want to go for a ride?' he asked, and lost his heart to her all over again when she looked at him with such pleasure in her eyes.

'Could we? I'd need to borrow some boots, though.'

Lance smiled at her enthusiasm. 'A pair of Rachel's should fit you. You'll need a hat, too.'

'Won't your sister mind me borrowing her things?'

'Nope. But just in case, we won't tell her. Come on up to the house and I'll rustle something up for you.' He turned and took a few steps back towards the house, then stopped and glanced over his shoulder when he heard her giggling. 'What?'

Kari had just noticed how he was dressed. His shirt was only half buttoned, and raggedly tucked into his jeans which were zipped but unfastened. 'You…ah…seem to have dressed in a hurry,' she observed when she could get a word out, and Lance glanced down at himself, a wry smile tugging at his mouth.

'I did, didn't I?' he agreed, combing his fingers through his sleep-mussed hair, then tucking in his shirttails.

Kari's stomach lurched. There was dark stubble on his unshaven jaw which gave him a decidedly rakish look. He was so sexy her heart rate increased and her blood raced through her veins. Her eyes found the tanned expanse of chest where his shirt was undone and her fingers itched with the urge to trace their way across his silky skin.

'Don't look at me like that, princess, not unless

you want me to make love to you right here on the ground,' Lance warned huskily, his body heating up at the look in her eyes. She didn't have to touch him to turn him on. 'I want to make love to you so damned much, but I promised myself I wasn't going to touch you until everything was settled between us,' he added in a sexy growl that raised the hairs all over her skin.

Kari flushed but her chin went up, and there was a martial light in her eye. 'Settled? Don't you mean when you've changed my mind about marrying you?' she countered, and he smiled wryly.

'I would be a liar if I said I didn't want to do that. I love you. Surely you know that means I would never deliberately hurt you?'

Her throat closed over. Of course she knew that. It had never been in doubt. 'Life has a way of inflicting its own wounds,' she said unevenly.

'It also provides the means of healing them,' he countered softly. 'Let me ease your pain, princess.'

Her heart lurched. 'Can you? How can I be sure?'

Lance brushed his knuckles along the gentle curve of her jaw. 'You can't, honey. You just have to want to believe. It's an act of faith,' he said throatily.

Her lashes dropped. 'I don't know that I have that much faith left in me.'

'Then use mine. I have enough for both of us,' he offered with a smile, then made a conscious effort to lighten the mood. 'Come on, time's a wastin'. We'll get you kitted out, then I'll saddle the horses. A long ride will do us both good. It's too fine a day to waste it feeling blue.'

He strode off towards the house, leaving Kari to follow a few paces behind. She stared after him, biting her lip. She knew he was right. Loving was an act of faith. You trusted that you wouldn't get hurt. Turning away from Lance hadn't taken away her pain, it had given her just as much. That had to be telling her something.

CHAPTER TEN

THEY rode for miles, and it was wonderful. The breeze took Kari's hair and whipped it out behind her, and the sense of freedom that simple action gave her was priceless. She found herself laughing aloud from sheer pleasure. This was what she had missed so much, and Lance had given it back to her. If she could only take her courage in both hands, he could give her so much more. She watched him riding beside her, so tall and strong, and for the first time she asked herself: dare she?

The sun rose higher, and after a while they rested the horses by a stream that ran through a small grove of trees. Lance produced cheese, crackers and fruit from a bag he had slung from his saddle, and they ate an alfresco breakfast resting back against a large tree trunk.

'It's so peaceful here.' Kari sighed when she had eaten her fill.

'I touch base at the ranch as often as I can,' Lance responded, stretching out his length on the grass. 'It helps me wind down.'

Kari chewed on a blade of grass, her gaze lost in the middle distance. 'You're lucky to have a place like this to come to.'

Lance folded his hands behind his head and closed his eyes. 'We all have something like it. Another person would seek out the ocean. For you it's your horses. They ground you, give you the peace you need. You lost sight of it for a while, but it's back now.'

'Thanks to you,' she responded, smiling faintly. He seemed to be always giving, and not asking for anything in return. He did it because he knew it would please her. It made her feel humble. She was always so worried about being hurt, she was afraid to give. It wasn't fair, because he deserved more. 'I'm grateful. Truly.'

'Does that mean you forgive me for tricking you into coming here?' he asked, tipping his head round so that he could see her. She looked relaxed and happy, and that alone made it worth it.

Kari looked at him askance. 'I haven't decided yet. It was a pretty rotten trick.'

'Done with the best of intentions.'

'Maybe,' she allowed grudgingly.

Lance lay back and closed his eyes again. 'We could be happy together, princess, if you'd just give us a chance.'

Her eyes roved over his relaxed figure, and she frowned faintly. The statement didn't arouse her fears the way she would have expected. 'Would we?'

'I'm not omnipotent. I can't see what lies ahead of us any more than the next man. I know I'd do my damnedest to look after you and make you happy. Beyond that, whatever happens happens. I believe that together we can deal with anything that comes along,' Lance responded with conviction, and Kari drew her legs up, wrapping her arms around them.

'You sound so…sure of everything,' she murmured, almost to herself, yet he heard her.

'That's because I feel empowered by my feelings for you, not diminished. Only life can prove me wrong, and I refuse to hide from it.'

As she had been doing, she acknowledged silently, and her lips twisted. 'You make me sound very weak.'

Lance rolled onto his side and met her eyes, holding them. 'Honey, you are so wrong. You know what they say: ''What doesn't destroy us, makes us strong''.'

'You think I'm strong?' she queried in surprise, and he nodded.

'You're here, aren't you? Life hasn't been kind to you, but you've made it this far. You had to be strong to do that on your own. But you aren't alone any more, honey. You have me, and whatever it is that you're afraid of we can beat it together. Don't you see that?' he urged in an impassioned undertone, willing her to believe it.

She said nothing, but he saw her frown and knew that at least she was thinking about it. He took it as a good sign and lay down again. He could only sow the seeds and hope they fell on fertile ground. If they didn't… Well, he'd cross that bridge when and if he had to. Closing his eyes, he allowed the warmth of the day to drift over him and draw him into the light edges of sleep.

Kari glanced his way when he had been quiet for some time, and sighed wistfully when she saw the rhythmic rise and fall of his chest which told her he was asleep. She had thought it would be better to hurt now rather than later, but it didn't make it any less painful. She loved him and it hurt not to be with him. The irony was, it was a self-inflicted wound. He hadn't sent her away, she had denied him. It had sounded so reasonable before, but now she wasn't so sure. The worst might never happen, but she would never know that if she refused to take a risk.

It was really very simple, she realised now. She had two choices. She could take the coward's way out—or she could take a chance on love. Give in to her fears, or take the happiness she knew in her heart she could have with this man. There were no guarantees in life, but there was love. There was always love.

Another half-hour passed before Lance awoke. His first instinct was to look for Kari. She wasn't sitting against the tree where he had last seen her, and he glanced round hastily, relaxing instantly when he saw her talking to her horse. A smile spread across his face as he saw the horse responding with a nod. Climbing to his feet, he dusted himself down with his hat, then set it at a jaunty angle on his head and went to join her.

'I take it you speak horse,' he said teasingly, reaching past her to stroke the blaze on the chestnut's head.

Kari was startled by his silent approach, and her head shot round. She was going to have to tie bells to him or he was going to scare her out of a year's growth! There was grass caught in his hair, and automatically she reached up to remove it.

'Don't you?' she quipped back, her heart lurching a little as she realised how settled the thought had been. As if her mind was made up.

'Not as well as you do, obviously,' he declared wryly. 'Are you ready to go? Do you want me to give you a leg up?'

Kari shot him an old-fashioned look. 'I can manage, thank you,' she refused primly. 'I've heard of men like you. You'll use any excuse to get your hands on a woman's body.'

He grinned. 'Darn it. Foiled again.'

Easily swinging into the saddle, Kari looked down on him from her superior height. 'I'm onto you now, Kersee. You'll never trick me so easily again!' she crowed, laughing.

Catching hold of her reins, he prevented her from leaving. 'Will I have the opportunity to try?' he asked, striving for lightness when his heart had taken to thumping a little faster.

Seeing the hopeful gleam in his grey eyes, Kari sobered. 'I don't know. Maybe,' she answered honestly, but it was enough for him.

'I'll always take maybe over a definite no,' he retorted, releasing her reins and mounting his own horse. 'It's good to see you smile again, princess,' he told her gruffly before turning his horse and urging him into a trot.

Kari followed, wondering if the limb she had just ventured out on was sound or not. One way or another, she was going to find out.

When they got back to the ranch house, Kari went to dismount and had to smother a groan. She hadn't ridden for so long, the unaccustomed riding had stiffened her up.

'What you need is a long hot bath,' Lance advised with a sympathetic wince as he dismounted and came round to help her down.

He swung her out of the saddle easily and Kari's hands went to his shoulders as he let her slide slowly to the ground. Her heart set off at a mad pace, but she didn't step away; instead she stayed where she was with his hands on her waist and stared up into his beautiful eyes.

'Do you have any idea how afraid I am to love you?' she asked unevenly, and Lance very nearly stopped breathing.

His hands tightened on her waist but she didn't seem to notice. 'Tell me,' he invited softly.

Kari looked down to where her hands rested on his chest. 'I never wanted to fall in love again. I swore I never would, but I didn't count on you. I tried to ignore you, but you wouldn't be ignored.' Her smile fluctuated and disappeared. 'Finding myself loving you was my worst nightmare,' she added huskily.

Lance felt as if he had been picked up and put down in a minefield. One wrong word and the whole thing would blow up in his face. He had waited for so long for this moment, it was vitally important he did nothing wrong. 'I've been called many things, but never that,' he responded softly, and saw the way her lips trembled before she pressed them together determinedly.

'I am so very terrified of losing you,' she confessed in a ragged whisper. 'I've had my heart broken once already, Lance. I felt it snap in two with the pain. I don't think I could bear to be hurt like that again. That's why I'm so afraid of loving you, because I couldn't bear to lose you.'

Lance's arms went around her and he pulled her close. In the next instant his heart twisted as he felt her arms slide around his waist. 'You aren't going to lose me, princess.'

'It scares me so much.'

Lance closed his eyes and rubbed his cheek against her hair. 'Honey, it's the same for me. I don't know if anything is going to happen to take you away from me. I do know that any time I spend with you is better than being apart from you. Life is too short for that.'

She knew he was right. They could have many happy years together if she would only take the risk. Wouldn't she regret it all her life if she didn't? The sky might fall in, but it hadn't yet. She had to trust that it never would.

'Hold me,' she pleaded urgently and his arms tightened around her.

She felt the solid strength of him and let her head rest on his shoulder. He felt so safe, she wanted to believe nothing would happen to him. That she could dare to love him and have a future with him. As he had said, wanting to believe it was the place to start.

'I love you,' she whispered, barely audibly.

Lance's heart threatened to burst out of his chest, and his throat closed over at the soft yet priceless confession. 'I love you too, princess. I love you too.'

'I never meant to hurt you,' she sighed, her fingers curling into his shirt and holding on tight.

He smiled. 'I knew that.'

She closed her eyes, breathing him in. He smelt so good. 'Nothing seems so bad with your arms around me.'

'Then I'll just have to keep on holding you,' Lance declared huskily, knowing it would be no hardship. In fact, it would be a pleasure. 'Thank you,' he added softly, and she tipped her head back, frowning faintly.

'For what?'

He pressed a kiss to each eye in turn. 'Trusting me enough to say you loved me. I know it wasn't easy for you. After forty or fifty years, you'll probably get the hang of it,' he teased gently.

She laughed a little shakily, burrowing her head against his heart. 'That long?'

'Longer if I can manage it.'

'You don't ask for much, do you?'

'Just your love for the rest of your life.'

Kari's heart thudded against her chest. How could she ever have considered spending the rest of her life without this man? His love, his faith and trust, would keep the fear at bay. 'You have it.'

Lance cupped his hands around her face and tipped her head up. 'If I ask you to marry me now, will you say yes?' he asked seriously.

Kari felt her heart flutter anxiously, then she looked deep into his eyes and saw all the love he had for her reflected there. Just believe, she told herself. Just believe. 'Ask me.'

He checked her face for doubts but could find none. 'Will you marry me, Kari Maitland?'

Her lips curved into a beautiful smile. 'Yes,' she breathed, and felt the last of her fears fade away. 'Oh, yes.'

'I'll do everything I can do to make sure you never regret it,' Lance promised thickly, and she lifted her hand to his cheek.

'I know you will. I've never for a second doubted you loved me.'

Lance drew in a long deep breath and turned his head enough to press a kiss into her palm. Everything was going to be all right. 'Does this mean you no longer think of me as scum and slime?' he teased with a glint in his eye, and Kari looked up at him, her cheeks a becoming shade of pink.

'If that stung it was your own fault. You lied to me.'

His eyebrow rose. 'I think you enjoyed cutting me down to size,' he returned and was delighted when she grinned.

'I still do.'

'I'd paste your delightful little butt for that if it wasn't sore already,' Lance retorted, grinning back, then bent quickly and hooked an arm under her legs, sweeping her into his arms.

'Where are you taking me?' Kari demanded breathlessly as he strode towards the house.

'To my bed. We've done talking, princess. I intend to take my time making slow, passionate love to you. Unless you have any objections, that is?' he asked, eyebrow raised questioningly.

Kari sighed and buried her face against his neck. 'I've no objections. No objections at all,' she said softly, and as he continued on his way she knew that she had come home at last.

The world's bestselling romance series.

HARLEQUIN®
Presents

Seduction and Passion Guaranteed!

GREEK TYCOONS

They're the men who have
everything—except a bride…

Wealth, power, charm—what else could
a heart-stoppingly handsome tycoon need?
In the GREEK TYCOONS miniseries you have
already been introduced to some gorgeous
Greek multimillionaires who are in need of wives.

THE GREEK TYCOON'S SECRET CHILD
by Cathy Williams
on sale now, #2376

THE GREEK'S VIRGIN BRIDE
by Julia James
on sale March, #2383

THE MISTRESS PURCHASE
by Penny Jordan
on sale April, #2386

Pick up a Harlequin Presents® novel and you will
enter a world of spine-tingling passion and
provocative, tantalizing romance!

Available wherever Harlequin books are sold.

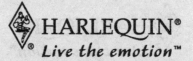

HARLEQUIN®
Live the emotion™

Visit us at www.eHarlequin.com

HPGT2004

The world's bestselling romance series.

HARLEQUIN®
Presents

Seduction and Passion Guaranteed!

Mama Mia!

They're tall, dark…and ready to marry!

Don't delay, pick up the next story in
this great new miniseries…pronto!

On sale this month
MARCO'S PRIDE by Jane Porter #2385

Coming in April
HIS INHERITED BRIDE by Jacqueline Baird #2385

Don't miss
May 2004
THE SICILIAN HUSBAND by Kate Walker #2393

July 2004
THE ITALIAN'S DEMAND by Sara Wood #2405

Pick up a Harlequin Presents® novel and you will
enter a world of spine-tingling passion and
provocative, tantalizing romance!

Available wherever Harlequin books are sold.

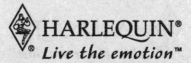

HARLEQUIN®
Live the emotion™

Visit us at www.eHarlequin.com

HPITHUSB

**If you're a fan of sensual romance
you *simply* must read…**

The third sizzling title in Carly Phillips's *Simply* trilogy.

"4 STARS—Sizzle the winter blues away with a *Simply Sensual*
tale…wonderful, alluring and fascinating!"
—*Romantic Times*

Available in January 2004.

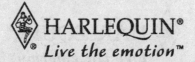

Visit us at www.eHarlequin.com

PHSSCP3

The world's bestselling romance series.

HARLEQUIN®
Presents

Seduction and Passion Guaranteed!

A gripping, sexy new trilogy from

Miranda Lee

THREE RICH MEN...

*Three Australian billionaires—they can have anything,
anyone...except three beautiful women....*

Meet Charles, Rico and Ali, three incredibly wealthy friends all
living in Sydney, Australia. Up until now, no single woman has
ever managed to pin down the elusive, exclusive and eminently
eligible bachelors. But that's about to change, when they fall
for three gorgeous girls....

But will these three rich men marry for love—
or are they desired for their money...?

Find out in Harlequin Presents®

A RICH MAN'S REVENGE—Charles's story
#2349 October 2003

MISTRESS FOR A MONTH—Rico's story
#2361 December 2003

SOLD TO THE SHEIKH—Ali's story
#2374 February 2004

Available wherever Harlequin® books are sold

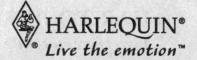

HARLEQUIN®
Live the emotion™

Visit us at www.eHarlequin.com

HSR3RM2

National Bestselling Author

brenda novak

COLD
FEET

Despite the cloud of suspicion that followed her father to his
grave, Madison Lieberman maintained his innocence...*until* crime
writer Caleb Trovato forces her to confront the past once again.

**"Readers will quickly be drawn into this well-written,
multi-faceted story that is an engrossing, compelling read."**
—*Library Journal*

Available February 2004.

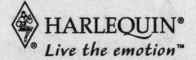

HARLEQUIN®
Live the emotion™

Visit us at www.eHarlequin.com

PHCF

The world's bestselling romance series.

HARLEQUIN®
Presents

Seduction and Passion Guaranteed!

Legally wed, great together in bed,
but he's never said…"I love you."

They're…

Wedlocked!

The series
in which
marriages are
made in haste…
and love
comes later…

Don't miss

THE TOKEN WIFE by Sara Craven,
#2369 on sale January 2004

Coming soon

THE CONSTANTIN MARRIAGE by Lindsay Armstrong,
#2384 on sale March 2004

**Pick up a Harlequin Presents® novel and you will
enter a world of spine-tingling passion and
provocative, tantalizing romance!**

Available wherever Harlequin books are sold.

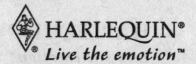

HARLEQUIN®
Live the emotion™

Visit us at www.eHarlequin.com

HPWEDJF